The One Inside the Looking Glass

Brieanna Robertson

Whimsical Publications, LLC

Florida

The One Inside the Looking Glass is a work of fiction. Names, characters, and incidents are the products of the author's imagination and are either fictitious or are used fictitiously. Any resemblance to actual events or persons, living or dead, is entirely coincidental.

If you purchased this book without a cover, you should be aware that this book may have been stolen property and reported as "unsold and destroyed" to the publisher. In such case, neither the publisher nor the author has received payment for this "stripped book."

To purchase the authorized electronic edition of *The One Inside the Looking Glass*, visit
www.whimsicalpublications.com

Cover art by Traci Markou
Editing by Shyanne England

ISBN-13: 978-1-940707-30-3

Published by
Whimsical Publications, LLC
Florida

"And do you want this job that badly?" For the
**first time, his voice actually rose in ferocity. "No
matter what the cost?"**

"Yes!"

"Then friggin' *fight* for it! You want it so badly, yet you
are willing to throw it away because of some petty fear? Do
you know how to fight for *anything*? Is there anything that
you would go to lengths for? Throw away your own selfishness for?"

"I'm not selfish!" she cried, but her voice wavered and
her chin trembled.

"Aren't you? You won't fight for anything—your husband,
your job...all these things you claim are important to you. Yet
here you are, whining about doing the SkyJump. You say you
are hungry for something, yet when it threatens you, you
decide to throw it away. If that's how you function, I'm not
surprised that your husband wants nothing to do with you."

Something exploded inside of Alyssa like a powder keg,
and she stabbed her finger into Hat-man's chest. "You think I
don't know how to fight for anything? You think nothing matters to me?"

He shrugged flippantly.

"Watch me," she growled. She turned on her heel and
strode toward the entrance to the SkyJump. She didn't think
about the height, didn't think about the drop, didn't think
about anything other than proving the obnoxious man in the
stupid hat wrong.

Because he had to be wrong. She wasn't selfish. She
wasn't.

She barely felt the man strapping her into her harness.

She had to prove them wrong, all of them. She wasn't
selfish; she was being responsible. She had to prove to
Tucker that *he* was wrong.

*Why is he the one who's wrong? He's happy. What are
you? A disaster.*

"Are you ready, miss?"

She stared straight ahead and thought of Tucker, of the
light in his beautiful blue eyes that had never died. Her eyes
had lost that light a long time ago. Now, when she looked in
the mirror, she only saw fatigue and dark circles.

"Miss?"

But that would change when she landed this job. She would be calling a lot of the shots. She wouldn't be an errand girl anymore, jumping through hoops all the time. She would finally be able to do something with her life, her dreams. She could get her life back together. All of this would be worth it then.

"Miss?"

Tucker would see. She hadn't abandoned their dreams together; she was making it possible for them to live their dreams. He would be able to act and not have to wait tables anymore. She could be the breadwinner, and in the process, she would be able to live her dreams as a designer. That was how it had to be. It was the only conclusion that made sense. She had been sacrificing all this time so that they could finally reach the goals they had set!

Tucker achieved his goals long ago. You ditched yours because you got discouraged. He's doing what he loves, and he's good at it. He's even working two nights a week as a sous chef for a prestigious restaurant. When he never even went to culinary school. He had the drive. He had the ambition. The only thing you're good at doing is blaming everyone else.

"Miss!"

"Just do it. Get it over with," she muttered.

"Um....well, you have to jump. It's not like I'm going to push you."

Alyssa glanced at the young man, then down at all the rigging he had strapped her into. She looked over at the platform she had to jump from, and instead of feeling terrified like she expected, she just felt numb. The war in her own mind switched off and she thought if she jumped, at least she wouldn't have to think for a couple of seconds. At the moment, that seemed like heaven...not thinking...not feeling anything.

She turned and leapt.

Without any thought. Without any fear.

She just...did.

ACKNOWLEDGEMENTS

To "overturning furniture," "little brother," "I have to pee,"
"I wanna dance my brains out!" "I love steak and eggs,"
"Walk in circles then!" "Instant Human," and
"No one touches my Mad Hatter's hat but me."
In other words, to those epic few,
And that epic weekend.

Also by
Brieanna Robertson

Chapter One

Alyssa sighed as she spoke to her husband Tucker on the phone. "No, I'm not going to be able to make it... I'm sorry... Tucker—" She waited while he ranted, angry and hurt that she couldn't make it to the Opening Night performance of his play. She couldn't really blame him. He had been working on it for the last four months and wanted her to come see it. No one else mattered to him. And Opening Night to an actor was like prom to a teenage girl.

But here she was...blowing him off for a job interview.

The job interview of a lifetime.

The interview to be Senior Creative Director of *Fashion and Design of the Modern Woman* magazine, directly under the creator and president, Gwenna Vartz.

She felt terrible.

At the same time, she felt empowered.

This was her life, her dream. Tucker was living his as an actor—a community actor who never got paid. It was about time she started living hers.

"Tucker, this would mean the biggest pay raise ever. We would be okay with this. You could keep acting with this."

Well, that didn't make him happy. He started going on and on about how he would keep acting even if he was starving and living in the sewers, because he was an artist and would not give up his creative vision for corporate flash and flare. How he had always been fine with just the essentials so long as he could live his dream. How he had always been that way and would not change, because he believed in something.

"Okay. Okay! Tuck, that's not what I meant! I just meant we could be more comfortable this way!" Alyssa interjected. "We could not struggle so much."

"What's the struggle, Liss?" he asked. "Is it the fact that

we only live in a one-bedroom? A nice one, by the way. Is it the fact that, while I act, I make a living as a waiter? One who also moonlights as a sous chef two nights of the week, by the way. Is that it?"

Alyssa pondered his words and felt like a douche, because she knew Tucker was a good chef, and a good actor. But still...they would be so much more comfortable with a steady income. Her income. "No, Tuck. It's that we wouldn't have to eat noodles for lunch anymore. We could have a sandwich now and then...or Sushi! You know how much you love Sushi."

"Gimme a break, Liss." His voice was saturated with annoyance. "We could eat Sushi now. I could even freaking *make* you Sushi. You're exaggerating and you know it. We went to that freakin' swanky steakhouse just last week for that stupid dinner party your office put on...and we paid our own way, mind you. Your amazing corporation made us pay for our dinner! For *their* party! And you weren't even required to be there!"

She snorted. "It was because it was the ten year anniversary of—"

"Save it, Liss. We are not at poverty level. We get by just fine. The only reason *you* eat noodles every day for lunch is because it's the fastest thing you can stuff in your gob before you run back into your office and continue to slave away. We could go out to Sushi whenever we wanted. Italian or French even. Insufficient funds is not the reason we don't go out. The reason we don't go out is because you're always busy working overtime. We eat like poor people because neither one of us is ever home to make a decent meal we can share."

Alyssa scowled, knowing his "neither one of us" really meant just her. "It's my job, Tucker. It's not like I can help it. We have to pay the bills somehow." She sniffed dismissively.

"And we do. We pay them on time every month. You know, I *do* work. It's not like you're carrying the whole load here. This entire argument is ridiculous and invalid."

"It's not ridiculous! Maybe I don't want to only pay the bills every month. Maybe I want nice things! Ever think of that?"

He made a weird, choking noise in his throat. "No. I never realized you were so superficial."

"Nice, Tucker," she spat. "I never realized you were such

an ass."

He heaved a long-suffering sigh. "Alyssa, look...I barely see you as it is. I'm pretty sure there are some cast members at the theatre who think I don't really have a wife, that I just made her up. You're never around. This is not how we wanted our lives to be. What kind of a marriage do we have if we lead entirely separate lives? What makes you think that this job is going to make that better for us? You're going to have an even bigger workload. Unless...unless you *want* us to see even less of each other..."

"No!" Alyssa cried, then steadied her voice, trying to rein in sudden tears. "No, Tuck, that's not it."

There was a long moment of silence before Tucker finally sighed and said, "Do what you feel is right, Liss. You've always been the brains while I've always been the creative one, the crazy one. Do what you want."

And he hung up on her.

Just like that, he hung up on her.

Irritated, Alyssa turned to where she had been studying layouts of the magazine she so badly wanted to run.

Granted, that had never been her ambition. She had met Tucker in college, and the two of them had imagined a life together living like Bohemians amongst the arts. She recalled his words. *The creative one...* That hurt. She had always been just as creative as him, just in a different way.

But time happened. Time and life.

Tucker still lived like a Bohemian.

But she...

She had the opportunity of a lifetime staring her in the face.

She had been working for the past three years at *Fashion and Design of the Modern Woman*, and the CEO, Gwenna Vartz, had chosen her and two other women to be in the running for Senior Creative Director. In other words, Alyssa had two other people to knock out of the way before she got an insane pay raise and a title that would launch her into the big leagues.

She would finally make something of herself.

She had no desire to squelch Tucker.

She just had a desire to support Tucker, to support both of them. Maybe buy a new couch or go on a vacation. Buy a decent car. She wasn't superficial, but she didn't want to live in a 900-square-foot apartment for the rest of her life either. Especially in Los Angeles. That did not scream success.

"Liss! Gerry offered you a job today! You could be our new set designer! Leanne is leaving!" Tucker's elated words to her a week ago after he had come home from rehearsal. *"We could actually work together! It would be like we always wanted!"*

Set designer...for a community theatre...

She would make a fraction of what she did at *Fashion and Design*. She would be insane to accept Gerry's ridiculous proposal when she could go for what Gwenna Vartz was offering. Tucker was a dreamy-eyed idealist to see it any other way.

She had the bigger paycheck and the most responsibility. *She* was supporting their family.

She had to be the one to make the tough calls.

Because he was never going to.

He was going to cling onto his starving artist lifestyle with such ferocity she would never be able to make him see reason.

She shook her head to dismiss the entire conversation she had just had with her husband and glanced at the clock. It was two o'clock. Tucker would be at work until four, and then he had to go to his dress rehearsal. She had to be at a work meeting at six. She still had plenty of time to pour over the magazine layouts and brush up on her interior design skills by doing some practice sketches. Wouldn't hurt to draw up some fashion designs as well and orient herself with all the current trends. She would have to be on the ball with all aspects of the magazine if she was going to be running it alongside Gwenna.

Alyssa gathered up her things and headed toward the bedroom, deciding the bed would be her workspace so she could spread everything out.

She dumped her pile on the bed and headed back to their small bar for a glass of afternoon wine. The conversation with Tucker had set her nerves on edge; she needed to relax so she could concentrate.

She poured a glass of Merlot and went back to the bedroom, glancing at the framed picture on the nightstand of her and Tucker during their honeymoon. A pang shot through her heart at the thought that he was hurt by her ambition, and she wondered if the two of them even shared the same goals anymore. At one time, they had been so in sync with one another. Now, half the time, it felt like they didn't even live in the same world. Alyssa wondered when the man she had fallen so hard for had turned into such a stranger.

Setting her wine on the nightstand, Alyssa climbed onto the bed and started to arrange her workspace. She couldn't dwell on her issues with Tucker right now. She had other things she needed to focus on. Like getting this job.

Because she *would* get this job.

Chapter Two

"Alyssa, wake up! We're going to be late!"

Alyssa frowned and peeked her eyes open just as the curtains were yanked back and sunlight came streaming into the room. She groaned and flopped her arm over her eyes. "What the heck, man? I think I just turned to dust!"

"Sorry, but we have to go. We're going to be late!"

Alyssa forced her eyes open and blinked a few times, then sat up in bed just in time to see her co-worker—her competition—all but running out of the bedroom.

It took Alyssa a second to figure out what was going on. Her brain felt foggy and muddled, like she was having a hard time grasping onto any specific memory, but as her platinum-haired co-worker came flying back into the bedroom and threw her overnight bag at her, Alyssa remembered she was in a hotel suite with the two other girls who were in the running for the Senior Creative Director position. "Where's Susan?" she muttered as she set her bag aside and swung her legs out of bed.

"She left already. I'm telling you, we're going to be late! Hurry up and get ready!"

Alyssa thought it was insanely nice of Lindy to even wake her up. If Alyssa had kept on sleeping, she wouldn't have been much competition for anyone.

She wondered why she had spaced setting her alarm the night before. She didn't really remember much at all from last night. She barely remembered getting off the plane and checking into the hotel. Man, she really needed to stop drinking wine before she went to bed.

She wracked her brain for a second, feeling like she was trying to put a puzzle together, but the pieces were eluding her. She was in...Las Vegas. She was here for...the interview. The interview was...a race...a scavenger hunt designed to...to test their problem solving skills and efficiency. A tiny bit of the haze lifted and a sense of urgency slammed into Alyssa. She needed to go.

Now!

"Susan is already gone?" she shrieked. "Where is the itinerary?"

"On your bedside table. Come on, Alyssa! Pull your head out of your butt and focus!"

Alyssa shook her head and pushed her flyaway strands of dark hair out of her eyes as she grabbed the itinerary they had all been given. The race started this afternoon and they had the rest of the day and most of the night to complete their tasks. They had each been given a clue to start out. Once they figured out where the clue was leading them, they would have to accomplish a task. Once that task was accomplished, they would be given another clue, and so on until they ended up at their final stop, which would be their evaluation. There were two mandatory halts to the competition. One at four for an hour long lunch, and one at eight for an hour long dinner.

Their first clue was: *Our bodies are a product of what we eat and drink. What you wear can make your belly bulge, or it can make it shrink. Help both large and small dress for success in one of fashion's biggest countries.*

"Did Susan already figure out the first clue?" Alyssa called as she glanced at the clock. It was two in the afternoon. How had she slept so long? She never slept that long.

"I'm not sure. She may have just run out of here to intimidate us. At any rate, hanging out in the hotel suite is not getting me anywhere. I have to go, Alyssa. Some people wouldn't have helped you, but I wouldn't feel right if I won the job just because I got you out of the running by not waking you up. If I get this job, I want it to be because I deserve it. Not because I slit someone else's throat. Good luck!" And with that, Lindy blew out the door all platinum hair and long legs.

Alyssa liked Lindy. She was a vibrant and enthusiastic go-getter with a real passion for fashion. At times, Alyssa thought that Lindy was even hungrier for the job than she was, and not because of the pay or the prestige either. Just because she loved the magazine *that much*. If she had to lose—which she had no intention of doing—losing to Lindy wouldn't be that bad. Susan, on the other hand... Alyssa would set the building on fire before she let Susan be the Senior Creative Director of *Fashion and Design.*

Okay, maybe not, but that was how strongly she felt about Susan not getting the job. Susan was ruthless and had no qualms about throwing people under the bus to get where she needed to go. Alyssa intended to stay far away from her during this weird excursion.

Deciding there was no use in rushing if she had no idea where she was going, Alyssa pondered the clue while she took a quick shower.

Obviously, she was going to be dressing people. That seemed apparent. She could handle that. While interior design was her real forte, she appreciated fashion and had dabbled in creating her own clothing line for a short time before getting hired at the magazine. Working there had polished her knowledge of fashion, so she was confident she could make most anyone look good despite their body type.

Help both large and small dress for success in one of fashion's biggest countries.

As she threw on a pair of white slacks and a pale blue blouse, she mentally checked off places along the Strip that would not meet the criteria. There were many shopping malls, but none of them could be considered one of fashion's biggest countries. New York, New York could be the place to go, so she Googled it on her phone to see if there were any large shopping areas in that casino. There weren't. So, the USA was out.

Paris maybe?

Well, they had a lot of boutiques and shops for accessories, but nothing seemed equipped for what the task seemed to be hinting at.

She thought some more while she dried her chestnut-colored hair and pulled it back into a loose ponytail. It came to her while she was putting her makeup on.

Milan was one of fashion's biggest cities.

Milan was in Italy.

So was Venice.

The Venetian had one of the biggest shopping complexes in Vegas.

That was the only place it could be.

Once she had figured out her destination, Alyssa got a move on. She knew Susan had probably already figured it out, as well as Lindy. That was fashion 101. As of right now, she was completely behind and needed to get the lead out.

Alyssa grabbed her phone and went to shove it in her purse, then briefly debated calling Tucker to see how he was doing, and to tell him to break a leg tonight at the show. Annoyance came flooding back to her as she recalled their last conversation. She stuffed the phone back into her bag. She'd call him on her lunch break. Right now, she had more important things to worry about.

It was great that the hotel they were staying at was the Bellagio. It wasn't far from the Venetian and she could get there on foot if she hustled. Her head was killing her and she was in dire need of coffee, so she decided she would duck into a coffee shop along the way. Just because she was running behind and in last place at the moment, did not mean she was out of the running. At the end of this, they would all be evaluated on their performance, not just on who finished first. She could not think straight until she took care of this caffeine withdrawal, and thinking straight was imperative.

She found a small coffee place on the main floor of the Bellagio. She headed in with the intent on ordering the largest, strongest thing on the menu.

The man who came over to take her order made her stop in her tracks, made her overworking brain stop, made everything stop.

He was dressed in a forest green button-down shirt and rust-colored jeans, and he had a tan top hat over his wavy blond hair with several playing cards stuck inside the brim. His eyes—one green and the other an eerie red color—were framed by bright green eye shadow on the upper lids and bright blue underneath. It resembled a weird kind of David Bowie bandit mask, but somehow, it suited him, and something about him made her heart falter.

"What can I get for you, love?" he asked, his accent distinctly British, his voice devastatingly soft.

"Uhh..." Alyssa just stared at him, all of her motor functions vanishing.

He arched an eyebrow. "Did you lose your voice, love?"

She blinked a few times to try and get herself back in order, to try to get her brain working again. She shook her head. "Sorry, um..."

He grinned and she nearly melted to the floor.

"Oh my gosh! How many times have I told you, you cannot be back here, you lunatic!" A petite, mousy-looking brunette came from what Alyssa assumed was the bathroom. She crossed the cafe and went behind the counter, where she grabbed a water bottle and proceeded to beat the hat guy with it.

"Well, you weren't out here to take her order, now were you?" he retorted as he dodged her blows.

"Next you're going to start expecting us to cut you a check! You do not work here!"

"You're right," he said. "I just loiter here."

"For reasons no one understands! Now get out of here and let me do my job!"

He chuckled and moved out from behind the counter, but didn't leave.

"Ma'am?"

Alyssa jerked her attention away from the man and back to the girl. "Huh?"

"What would you like to order?"

"Oh...uhh...a large cafe mocha with an extra shot of espresso, please."

She went to make her order and Alyssa slid her gaze back over to the eccentric guy. She was startled to see him regarding her as well. It made her blood burn, and that made her uneasy. She shouldn't be feeling so turned on by a weird stranger.

He unleashed his devastating grin on her again. "See something you like, love?"

She felt her face flush with color. "You look like the Mad Hatter," she grumbled, trying to come off as snarky, but that just made him grin wider.

"Perhaps." He swept off his hat and bowed.

She raised an eyebrow and couldn't help smirking at his flamboyance. It reminded her of Tucker when she'd first met him. He had always been an outgoing person, but he'd walked the line between eccentric and downright nuts when they had been in college. She'd always admired his confidence and charisma, even his nuttiness. It had been so sexy to her.

"So, what, you just like to hang out in here and harass the staff? Is the coffee that good?"

He shrugged one shoulder. "Not really. I prefer tea myself."

She rolled her eyes, but her smirk widened into a smile. "Of course you do."

"I just like to create a little chaos now and again. Let's you know you're alive." He pointed to the cashier. "She loves me. She just doesn't know it yet. Rest assured, if I stopped coming in here, she would miss me."

"Whatever you say."

"And what brings you to Las Vegas, dear?"

"A job interview. Or, really, it's like a job scavenger hunt. It's this really weird test full of tasks and riddles."

"Oh? For what, might I ask?"

"Senior Creative Director of a magazine."

"I see. Well, it makes sense that the creative director of anything would need to be creative, thus the scavenger hunt. How are you doing so far?"

"Not so great. I'm running behind."

He made a tsk noise and shook his head. "It's never good to be late, dear."

"Yes, thank you for telling me what I already know. But that's all right. I'll make it up. This job isn't going to anyone but me."

"Stubborn," he stated.

"Ambitious," she countered.

"A rose by any other name..."

She peered at him through narrowed eyes and crossed her arms over her chest. "Call it what you will, but it gets the job done. This is my dream job. I *will* win."

"A dream job to sit in a corporate office? Sounds terribly dull to me."

"Yes, well, it would be a substantial raise in pay. You know what? Why am I defending myself to you? I don't know you at all. Why I want this job is none of your concern." She turned back to face the counter.

"So good at dismissing people. I imagine you will be a good executive."

She spun back around to face him and opened her mouth to shoot back an angry retort. He spoke again before she could formulate the words.

"I like the fire in your eyes, love. Shows me you really do have passion for something. You haven't completely given up your life to the hamster wheel yet."

"The hamster wheel? The hamster wheel *is* life. It's called being an adult."

"Is that always what you wanted to do with your life? Be a corporate slave?"

Alyssa's chest felt tight all of a sudden. She couldn't tell if it was because she was flabbergasted, or if it was for some other reason she really didn't want to stop and explore. "No, I wanted to be a rootless artist, but everyone has to grow up," she spat. "There is no room for dreaming in the real world."

"And who told you that?"

She stared at him for a moment, speechless, addled by how easily this man was getting to her when she was usually pretty impervious to things of this nature, and by the compelling look in his bizarre eyes.

"Everyone needs to dream. Even adults need a good...fantasy now and again."

His gaze swept her from head to toe in a distinctly suggestive way; tingles broke out over her entire body. Her throat was suddenly very dry.

"Ma'am?"

Alyssa jolted back to the present and all but ran up to the counter to get her coffee. She felt completely unhinged and needed to get a grip. Her brain was all over the place today, and that was not going to be an asset during this competition.

"Hatter!" the mousy brunette shouted again. "Get *out* of here!"

Alyssa turned back to the man, and a laugh was torn from her throat. "They actually call you that?"

He gave her a bemused expression. "Well, of course they do. I'm wearing a hat."

More laughter bubbled up from her chest, easing the tightness she'd been experiencing. "And do you have a real name?"

He pinned her with his gaze again then gave her a mischievous smirk. "Yes," he stated in a way that let her know he had no intention of telling her.

She smiled in spite of herself and shook her head. "I have to go. I've blown enough time already." She started out the door.

"And what is this first task you must accomplish?" he asked, following after her.

"I have to dress three people fashionably over at the Venetian."

"May I be of assistance?"

She glanced over him incredulously as they continued to walk. "I really don't think you would be much help to me in the fashion department."

"Oh-ho-ho, look who turned into a judgy judgerton. You might be surprised at what tricks I have up my sleeve."

Though his constant lightheartedness was easing away all of that terrible tension she'd been experiencing, she couldn't have him tagging along with her. He would be way too much of a distraction. "Maybe I would, but I'm pretty sure having help is against the rules. They might offer you the job instead of me." She flashed him a teasing smile.

"A valid point. All right, then here is where we say adieu, my dear. Thank you for brightening my afternoon."

He stopped keeping stride with her and she paused to turn back to him, warmed by his words. In truth, he had brightened hers too, even if he'd exasperated her with his nettling. It felt good to banter. She'd used to tease that way all the time with Tucker, but they never did anymore. Now all they did was argue.

"Thanks to you as well, Mr. Hat-man."

"Do you have a name?"

She hesitated, then decided there was absolutely no harm in him knowing her name. "I'm Alyssa."

A grin blossomed across his face. "Of course you are. Well, have fun here in Wonderland, *Alyssa*." He swept off his hat again, made a grand bow, then met her gaze for a brief moment, his eyes full of mirth and mystery. Then, he turned and strode away.

She pondered his words, then laughed softly to herself. She'd never realized how close her name was to Alice, and meeting the "Mad Hatter" was most definitely an ironic coincidence. Especially in a place like Las Vegas, which was a Wonderland all of its own.

Chapter Three

As luck would have it, Alyssa managed to pass a shop in the Grand Canal Shops at the Venetian right as Lindy was running out. Alyssa was relieved because it cut off the amount of time she would take trying to find the right store, which cut her running behind time margin in half at least.

She headed into the store and went to the first person who looked like she knew what she was doing—a tall woman with a severe ponytail and a scowl like no tomorrow. "I'm Alyssa Drake. I'm here to 'dress both large and small for success.'"

The woman raised a dark eyebrow, her only display of emotion, and beckoned three women over to her. One was rotund, one was stick thin with no chest or hips to speak of, and the other had a classic hourglass figure with more hips than boob. "These are your people. Bring each final outfit by me to pass inspection."

Alyssa stared for half a second. It would have been better if the woman had a Russian accent, but she didn't. Upon receiving no further instruction, she turned to the rotund one. "You. Over here."

The woman ambled over to her, boobs in a poor bra swinging away, and ample muffin top bulging out over way too small jeans.

Alyssa suppressed a cringe. "Hi. Come with me." She snatched the woman's wrist and yanked her over to a section of clothing that would work with her body type. She grabbed several items, ignoring any protest the woman was making. This was about her job interview, not about this woman's terrible style choice. Finally satisfied with her ensemble, she shoved it in the woman's hands and demanded she go try it on.

The woman emerged moments later in an A-line black skirt and a chic floral print blouse cinched with a thin black belt that accentuated her natural waist. Pointed-toe black heels polished the look. Alyssa smirked with confidence.

The woman stood in front of the mirror, scowled, then turned on Alyssa with rage in her eyes. "I look ridiculous!" she hollered.

Alyssa frowned in confusion. How could she think that when she looked markedly better than her former dumpy t-shirt, jeans, and flip-flops? "Excuse me?"

"I look like every rich, annoying, hoity-toity idiot who has ever gone through a pair of double doors."

Alyssa blinked at her, taken aback. She looked around to see if any personnel were coming to aide her and tell the woman her time as a model was over and it was time to move on.

No one did.

"If you're supposed to be the person to tell me that *this* is high fashion, I am liable to stop reading your magazine alto-gether," the redneck woman twanged.

That set off Alyssa's warning bells. Losing readers was the first step into getting fired. Loss of readership would not be tolerated. "Okay! Okay!" she cried in panic, then took a deep breath to calm her nerves. "What don't you like about it?"

"How about...everything?" the woman snarled. "I am a stay-at-home mom. I have been barefoot and pregnant for the last ten years of my life. Tell me how *this* look is going to get me anywhere."

Alyssa swallowed because the lump in her throat was al-most as bad as the tightness in her chest she felt earlier. "Well...it denotes a level of successfulness, and that is some-thing all women—"

"Seriously?" she hissed. "You think that this denotes suc-cess? As a stay-at-home mom? You want me to wear this? At home? Where my three-year-old can spill juice on it and my newborn can spit up all over it? You want me to play outside with my seven-year-old in a skirt and blouse? A skirt and blouse that costs more than my rent? That's successful in your world? Because I'll tell you what, success is raising four children to not be psychopaths in this jacked up world. *That's* what success is."

The suffocating feeling started to come back to Alyssa. "Okay, okay..."

"Raising four children to be *proud* of themselves and to not feel inferior because other girls and boys have better clothes and bigger homes is success!"

"Okay!" Alyssa cried.

"Having food on the table on time so your children don't go hungry is way more important than getting up in the morning and putting on some stupid outfit that has no use in your life! *That's* success!"

The random humming in Alyssa's ears made it difficult to think. She held her hands out in front of her in a plea to stop. "Okay, I get it!" Finally, the woman stopped her tangent. When Alyssa felt like she could breathe again, she opened her eyes—which had been squeezed tight. Her insides felt weird and squirmy, uncomfortable, and when she looked at the woman, it was like she had seen her for the first time. She *didn't* look right in the outfit. She looked lost and out of place, like a sad excuse for a doll someone had decided to play dress up with.

Drawing a deep breath, Alyssa met the woman's hazel-eyed gaze. It was the first time she had noticed that her eyes were hazel. And her hair was bleached blonde, but had long since grown out, showing about three months' worth of brown roots. The woman undoubtedly had no time to re-color her hair while trying to corral four rugrats. She proba-bly barely had time to breathe. An image flashed in Alyssa's mind of this woman trying to chase after a naked toddler in the pointed-toe shoes she was currently wearing. She'd probably trip on a baby toy and break her ankle.

"What is your name?" she asked with a sigh.

The woman looked bewildered for a moment before re-plying, "Dawn."

Alyssa nodded. "All right, Dawn. Why don't you tell me about yourself? Tell me about your family and about what you would like your style to reflect. You obviously signed up for this for a reason."

"Yeah, I signed up for this because I was promised a thou-sand dollar shopping spree at the end of it." And then Dawn proceeded to tell Alyssa all about her husband and four chil-dren. How they were barely scraping by, and how she desperately wanted to dress like an adult again, to feel desirable again, and not have to wear stained t-shirts and track suits every day of her life. She wanted to take some time for herself when she was used to giving one hundred percent to her family.

Alyssa couldn't help but replay the argument with Tucker the night before. She had claimed they were barely getting by, but she looked like a millionaire compared to this woman.

With Dawn's input, Alyssa managed to dress her in a practical pair of jeans that fit her correctly and a low-maintenance blouse that made sense with her everyday life, but had enough flare to make her feel like herself and not just like "a mom." The clothing was casual, but fit her body properly, which went a long way in making her look better.

When Dawn looked in the mirror, she actually squealed with delight, which made a strange thrill run up Alyssa's body. "So, do you like this?" she questioned.

Dawn turned to her with tears in her eyes and grasped her hands. "If you can find me another outfit like this, I want *you* to dress me for my shopping spree."

For whatever reason, her words made Alyssa feel like she had won the lottery. She promised to find Dawn another outfit—despite the time crunch—and whichever one she liked the best, she could model for the ponytail girl.

Dawn chose the first one, even though the second outfit—a teal button-down shirt and a casual yet flattering walking short—still fit her and her lifestyle well.

Alyssa supported her choice, then headed for the skinny girl. Without wanting to make the mistake she had made with Dawn, she ignored her impulse to dress her immediately in a high-waist pencil skirt and blouse. Instead, she sat down with her and said, "Hi, I'm Alyssa. What's your name?"

She said her name was Amy, and she fancied "Boho Chic" as her style choice. She said she was an artist and preferred to dress in nonconventional things that were flowy and eccentric.

Alyssa had to tap into her inner Tucker—and a dormant part of her old self—to find the proper dress for Amy, but she was confident she did so, sending her to the stylist-judge when they had both come to a happy agreement.

The third girl was easy. She was named Natalie and had

a classic pin-up girl shape. As luck would have it, that's the style she gravitated toward, so that was a win-win all the way around.

When she had finished, the woman with the ponytail gave Alyssa her second clue, which read: *You've accomplished your first task, but don't let yourself get too big for your britches—you may find your head in the clouds. Are you ready to prove your hunger by taking the plunge?*

As Alyssa left the store, she barely registered the cryptic message. Her mind was still on what had just occurred. She felt accomplished and on top of the world, yet somehow bothered.

She slowed her pace at the door that would lead her back out onto the Strip, not yet knowing where she was headed. She felt like her chest was going to explode. She put her hand over her wildly beating heart and took several deep breaths, trying to will the bizarre feeling to go away.

Dawn kept flashing in her mind, her story and the way Alyssa had initially treated her. It disturbed her on a level she didn't even understand. To know that woman had been desperate, had trusted her, and Alyssa had treated her like an object. "Dress for success" was about what "success" meant to each person and their life, not what society deemed as "trendy." That's what the whole magazine was about. The magazine she *worked for.*

Had she really become that shallow? That people were no longer people but things to use?

"So, how did it go?"

Alyssa jumped, barely stifling the shriek that threatened to erupt from her throat. The "Mad Hatter" stood before her, smirking, and she briefly wondered if she really had lost her mind.

She sighed, not even bothered by his presence. In fact, it seemed to soothe her. "It was...different than I imagined," she stated.

"Oh? How so?"

She arched an eyebrow toward him. "Did you follow me then wait out here like a freaky stalker?"

He put his hand over his heart and seemed theatrically affronted. "I was merely intrigued by your story. Can you fault me for such a thing?"

For some reason, she found that she couldn't, even if she normally would have. She waved it away, not caring why he was there, just strangely happy that he was. She glanced back down at her clue.

"So, tell me, why was it different than you imagined?" he prodded.

Alyssa heaved a sigh. "I thought it was going to be all about the fashion, the aesthetics. I thought I was going to be given some random model a casting company hired, but they were real women with real stories, like our readers. Turns out the task was more about listening than anything else, which makes sense. I mean, we need to cater to our audience... It just seems I don't listen as well as I thought." She mumbled the last part, ashamed and embarrassed.

Hat-man shrugged. "A common problem among women, I notice...even though they claim contrary."

She scowled furiously.

He chuckled and placed a hand on her shoulder. "Tell me, do any of us listen as we should? Did you learn something?"

She thought a moment then nodded slowly.

"And what was that?"

"That the outside surface doesn't matter if the inside is unhappy."

"Ah...a profound truth, love."

She briefly thought about Tucker, about the two of them. When they had gotten married, they hadn't cared about anything other than being together. Starting out after college, they had lived in a studio apartment, ate beans and weenies three nights a week, and had about ten articles of clothing between the both of them. Alyssa had never cared one iota about having to wash the same pair of jeans every single night, or about sharing a bathroom the size of a coat closet. She had gone to sleep every night in Tucker's arms, which was where home had always been to her. Everything else had just been extra.

When had that changed?

She knew when. After getting her job at the magazine.

An oppressive weight settled over her as she fidgeted with the clue she was staring at but not really seeing.

Was she really the reason that she and Tucker were unhappy now? That couldn't be right. Her job had brought them stability. Her job had made it possible for them to live in something other than a hovel. And if she received this promotion, they would be even more comfortable. Then it wouldn't matter if Tucker worked at all. He could spend all of his time doing theatre and living his dream.

She was doing this for them!

Tucker was the one who couldn't see that she was doing this to help them. He was the one being completely unreasonable.

"Are you stumped then?"

Alyssa jolted out of her random musings and glanced back up at Hat-man. "Huh?"

He pointed at the paper she was twisting around and mangling. "I wasn't sure whether you were angry at it or just hoped that wringing it out would procure an answer."

She shook her head and tried to smooth the paper back out. "No, I...I don't know what I was doing. Thinking, I guess."

"So that's what that burning smell was."

The look she gave him would have wilted a lesser man, but he just laughed and held his palms up. "Read me the clue, love."

"I really don't think that's a good idea. I'm not supposed to have help."

"Is that in the rules? Shouldn't a good executive know when to ask for help? Shouldn't she be able to utilize her team? Obviously, I can't do the tasks for you, but I am rather good with riddles. I figure, unless it was specifically mentioned in the guidelines of this silly quest, why not take advantage of me?" He raised his eyebrows and grinned, his statement heavily laden with double meaning.

Alyssa felt her cheeks burn again and she rolled her eyes, trying to shake off the effect he had on her. "Fine. Here." She shoved the paper up against his chest.

He looked down at the clue and read it over once. "Oh, well this is an easy one." He glanced back up at her as if she should have figured it out already.

She raised a questioning eyebrow.

He pointed at the paper. "You may find your head in the clouds? Prove your hunger by taking the plunge? The SkyJump at Stratosphere."

She stared at him, uncomprehending.

"It's easy, love. You go up to the hundred and eighth floor of the Stratosphere, jump off the top, plummet to your death, and then they slow you down at the bottom."

Alyssa's eyes bulged and her heart flipped dramatically, thundering against her ribcage. "I beg your pardon?" she wheezed.

"Yeah. Piece of cake. I've done it, I don't know, about four times. Feels like you're flying. It's a glorious sensation."

A wave of nausea passed over Alyssa and she wavered on her feet for a moment. "What...what kind of an insane test is that? What is that supposed to prove?"

"That you're willing to go to any length for your job, I would imagine." He reached out and took her elbow, steadying her. "Are you all right, dear? You look horribly pale all of a sudden."

"I...I'm really scared of heights," she rasped.

"Oh, well, now that could pose a problem."

"Wh-what time is it?"

He pulled a pocket watch, of all things, out of who knew where, and opened it. "Five to four."

She waved her hands, trying to dismiss the woozy feeling she had been experiencing. "I have to stop for lunch. We all do. I never ate breakfast. Maybe I need to eat something. Yeah. I should eat something."

"Are you sure eating is a good idea when you're about to drop a hundred stories in a freefall? I mean, your stomach is going to be up by your ears, so I'm not sure—"

"Dude." She fixed him with a look.

"Sorry. Food then?"

She nodded.

"I know just the place."

Chapter Four

The place Hat-man took her to was weird. It was some dismal, darkened dungeon of a place in between Treasure Island and Stratosphere—she wasn't sure where. It was down a back alley and in some creepy corner where she was pretty sure they were going to be raped and murdered. The fact that it was daylight outside, and inside it looked like an establishment vampires should frequent, did not put her at ease.

"What *is* this place?" she muttered as she fiddled with the menu.

"The Rabbit Hole," he stated.

She gave him a flat expression. "Of course it is."

He raised an eyebrow. "What?"

She sighed, ignored him, and wondered while she perused the menu if this guy was in possession of all his faculties.

"So...tell me about yourself," he stated suddenly.

She glanced up from the menu. "Excuse me?"

"Well, I'd like to know who it is I decided to assist, so tell me about yourself."

She flopped her menu down on the table, causing a *smack* sound. "Not sure entirely what you want to know." She folded her hands in front of her and stared him down.

His eyes narrowed. "Why do you do that?"

"What?" she asked in bewilderment.

"You shut people out like you are shutting a door. And you assume this cold, hard, bitchy exterior in order to maintain your aloof composure and make sure no one ventures closer."

She blinked at him, taken aback. She looked down at where her hands were clasped, like she was in a business meeting.

"Can I take your order?"

Alyssa glanced up at the waitress, who was wearing a

very short black skirt and red and white striped stockings. She stammered out her reply before turning her attention back to her hands. Did she approach all things like she had to assert her dominance? Like she had to win? When had she started caring about things like that? Was she really "bitchy?"

She slowly pulled her hands apart and let them fall to her sides, then wiped her palms on her thighs, feeling lost and awkward. She suddenly had an overwhelming desire to text Tucker.

She reached in her bag and fumbled for her phone, feeling the need for a tie to something normal. None of this so far had been anywhere near her realm of normal. She was sitting at a table in a dive called The Rabbit Hole—with the "Mad Hatter," who she was bizarrely attracted to—and the waitress looked like she'd come straight out of *Wizard of Oz*. If a house fell on her, Alyssa was done with all of this. So done.

She stabbed in a text, more angry than it should have been, saying that she was in the middle of the interview—not that he cared—and that she hoped his play went well. She stared at it for a minute, her finger hovering over the send button; instead, she deleted everything before *I hope your play goes well*. Why did she feel so confused about her husband? Why did nothing suddenly make any sense? Her emotions were raging out of control like a tropical storm.

"Who you texting?" Hat-man asked suddenly.

She glanced up at him with a scowl. "None of your business." She didn't intend to snap at him. She was really just upset at herself for not being able to get it together. He just happened to be there.

He let out a slow breath. "You *are* a cold one, aren't you?"

She frowned, feeling affronted. "What? I'm not—"

Their food came then and she took the opportunity to leave the conversation. She wasn't cold, she was focused. There was a difference. She had to be in her line of work. There was no room for error. The corporate world was cutthroat. A person had to be strong to survive it, a force to be reckoned with, a tigress. She had learned to adapt to that. Besides, how did she know this dude wasn't some worker for the company, sent to test her and see if she would lose that focus? Nothing seemed out of the realm of possibility in this bizarre goose chase.

You're acting like a lunatic.

She glowered at nothing and stabbed at her salad like it was the thing perturbing her.

And you really are being a little bit of a jerk. Did you pull on your bitch panties today instead of the big girl ones?

What was that? Her conscience? Great, maybe it would manifest itself in the form of a cricket with an umbrella. She wouldn't even be surprised. Besides, she wasn't bitchy; she was assertive. She was confident. She was—

"I hardly think the salad deserves such fierce punishment."

The reminder of his presence just fueled her confusion, and thus her irritation. He was throwing her nine ways off of her game! "If I want to stab my salad, I'll stab my salad. I'll do what I please when I please, and I don't need anyone, least of all a crazy stranger, telling me otherwise."

Way to lose your cool, Alyssa. That makes you look completely competent.

She bristled at the intrusion of that stupid, unwelcome voice. It was throwing her off even more than Hat-man was.

"Look, love, I'm not your enemy. Whatever you're so pissed off about, that's your own personal issue. I have done nothing but offer you assistance and kindness, so if you feel the need to attack someone or something, kindly aim your barbs elsewhere."

She glanced up at him in surprise. His voice had never risen above its velvety cadence, and he was still sitting relaxed and composed, but she felt as if she had been slammed into her place so hard she lost her breath.

She really was being a bitch.

For no reason at all.

Why?

Why did she want to lash out at this man? At Tucker? At anyone who had any sort of idea contrary to hers, or who tried to get her to see things any other way than what she knew? That wasn't her. That had never been her...had it? Why did it seem so difficult for her to put her old self and her current self together in one cohesive person? She suddenly felt so perplexed about everything. Nothing felt like it made sense.

She set her fork down slowly and looked at her white slacks—pristine, wrinkle-free, creased right where they were supposed to be with a line sharp enough to give someone a paper cut. She remembered a time when she wouldn't have been caught dead in something like that. She'd always preferred loose skirts with wild patterns and worn jeans. Now her closet was full of these—slacks—the corporate identification marker.

She wanted to think of herself as a business woman, but was she really? She always did someone else's business, never her own. And she wanted to think of herself as an artist, a creative person with an eye for design in both fashion and interior, but was she really? She spent all of her time designing what everyone else told her to, never her own ideas.

That would change if she got this job. Her opinion would matter. Her ideas would be looked at. Her voice would be heard. But she would never be able to land the job in her current state.

Still, her inability to get her crap straight was not this man's fault. She was taking it out on him because he was an easy target. It was easier to snap at him than at herself for suddenly not having her head screwed on correctly. "You're right," she said, more to her napkin than to him. She couldn't even bring herself to meet his gaze. "I'm sorry." There was a long pause, so long that she was forced to look up to see if he was even still there.

He arched an eyebrow, and a small, amused smile played around his lips. "Did that hurt you?" he questioned.

"Yeah, a little," she admitted. He chuckled, and she laughed softly, easing a bit. "I don't know what's wrong with me. I'm all rattled today. This job interview is really strange. I woke up late in my hotel, but I don't remember getting there. I must have drunk *a lot* of alcohol. I don't even remember saying goodbye to my husband...which would probably explain why I haven't heard from him."

"Your husband...that was who you were texting?"

She nodded. "Tucker. We had a fight before I left."

"About what?"

She rolled her eyes. "This job...life...I don't know. He can be kind of unreasonable sometimes." Even as she said it, guilt washed over her. Was he really the unreasonable one? If so, why did she have to keep reminding herself?

To Hat-man's credit, he didn't push the subject. Instead, he just pointed down to where she was twiddling with her mushroom salad. "You know, sometimes it is unwise to eat mushrooms."

It was such a direct and random statement that it caught her off guard for a moment. When she realized the reference to *Alice in Wonderland*, she couldn't help but laugh, and more of her tension dissolved. "Who are you exactly?" she asked as she met his gaze. "Are you an actor? Or are you a paranoid schizophrenic who actually does think he's the Mad Hatter?"

He gave a casual shrug. "Well, if I was a paranoid schizophrenic, I probably wouldn't know it, so I definitely wouldn't admit it to you." He smirked slyly. "I guess you'll never really know, will you?"

She smiled and let the subject drop. It didn't really matter. For reasons she didn't understand and was unwilling to look at too closely, he was the only thing that seemed to be keeping her grounded at the moment. Maybe she was having a nervous breakdown.

She shoved away her overwhelming desire to be rigid and shook her head. "I wasn't always like this, you know. I'm *not* always like this. I don't know why I can't seem to get my act together today."

"Maybe your act doesn't want to get together."

She looked up at him in confusion.

"Maybe your act has been together for too long."

She frowned. "I...I'm not sure what you mean by that. There is nothing wrong with having your act together. It's called stability. It's called—"

"Being an adult?" He grinned and shifted in his seat so that his hands were folded and he was leaning over the table slightly. "Yes, you've said that."

"Well, it is! There comes a point when you have to stop having pipe dreams, you know? You need to make a living somehow!" She fidgeted because she didn't know what else to do.

He regarded her calmly for a moment before he said, "For some people, pipe dreams are all they have. It's what keeps them going day to day. The ability to dream is what separates people from sheep."

She wanted to snap off a heated reply, but she stuffed her mouth full of salad instead. He did not deserve her venom; he was just voicing his opinion.

"I used to have pipe dreams," she muttered, lettuce falling out of her mouth, "but then I grew up and realized those dreams were never going to amount to anything. If I wanted a real life, I needed to get my head out of the clouds."

"And what constitutes a 'real life,' love? Seems to me a 'real life' shouldn't be something someone else tells you that you should have."

She dropped her fork with a clatter on her plate and suddenly felt like she was choking. Certain statements he made were like arrows that felt like they stabbed her straight in the part of her heart she tried to ignore all the time—the whimsical part, the part that had served next to no purpose in getting her anywhere in life, that loose skirts and worn jeans girl...the part that Tucker loved, or had loved anyway.

"You look pale," Hat-man observed. "Maybe you should have a drink or something. You seem a mite on edge."

"I can't drink on the job," she snorted.

"You're not on the job. You're on a strange interview, remember?"

"Still, I highly doubt that drinking myself into oblivion would be smiled upon when I make it to the end of this thing."

"Well, now, having *a* drink and drinking oneself into oblivion are on two entirely opposing ends of the spectrum." He motioned to their waitress, and before Alyssa could even register words spoken between the two, a glass of red wine had all but appeared on the table in front of each of them.

She blinked in bewilderment and glanced up at him, then gave him a bemused expression. "Isn't drinking wine almost as bad as eating mushrooms?" she asked dryly.

He wagged his eyebrows playfully as he lifted his glass and indicated hers. "Only one way to find out."

"You are the worst form of peer pressure ever..." She rolled her eyes and glanced at her wine glass. She felt like it was beckoning her. *Drink me. Calm your nerves. Take the edge off so you can think.* Maybe she was becoming an alcoholic. She didn't know. Part of her wondered what she was even doing here. This interview had not proceeded as she had imagined, and she hadn't even made it to the second task yet. She felt lost and alone—vulnerable—for the first time in a long time. She didn't like it, not one bit.

She heaved a deep sigh and grasped her glass. She fixed

Hat-man with a piercing stare. "If I lose this job because you made me drink wine, I will find you and kill you."

He tilted his head to the side and smirked. "Don't see anyone twisting your arm, love."

She narrowed her eyes then took a sip, closing her eyes as the red liquid flowed down her throat and filled her with what would soon be a soothing effect. "I don't know if I can do this Stratosphere thing," she admitted quietly. He said nothing and she glanced up to see him regarding her with a gentle gaze. "I went to an amusement park once with Tucker and he forced me to go on this roller coaster that went upside down and topsy-turvy. He loves the things. I threw up everywhere and almost passed out. It was awful."

"'Why is a raven like a writing desk?'"

She frowned. "I beg your pardon?"

"It's a Lewis Carroll quote... It just seemed appropriate somehow. If you can figure out the answer to that, it would be amazing, as I have been wracking my brain since I was twelve, but really, I just said it to distract you. You were getting a little morose and starting to doubt yourself." He flailed his hand in her direction. "Drink your wine, woman. You don't have much time left."

She glanced down at her phone. 4:45. She grabbed her wine glass and sucked down half the contents. "A raven is like a writing desk because a raven denotes death and darkness. So does a writing desk, because as soon as you sit down to try and write something, it dies," she rattled off. She took another gulp, and when he said nothing, she looked up at him.

His expression was slightly astonished. "Nice symbolism," he remarked.

She shrugged one shoulder. "Think about it. Everyone spends all of their time trying to scrutinize Lewis Carroll and say he was a drug addict. Maybe he was just a genius and maybe he just had writer's block. A writing desk would seem like death to an author with writer's block, don't you think?"

Hat-man stared at her, then nudged his half-full glass of wine toward her. "Maybe you should have some more because that was a little bit brilliant."

She waved her finger at him. "Oh no, Hat-man. If I have to drink mine, you have to drink yours. And seriously, why has no one ever thought of that before? It seems logical enough to me." She downed the rest of her glass then glanced at him. His amazing grin made her insides catch fire. She hated it because she shouldn't feel that for a stranger. She loved it because she hadn't felt it in far too long.

He drank the rest of his wine and called for the check. Again, faster than she could process, the waitress dropped it off and he paid it.

Alyssa stammered. "I could get my own lunch," she protested.

"And how much of a gentleman would I be if I let you?" he chastised. "I was, after all, the one who brought you here."

She studied him for a moment while he settled the bill. "What do you do exactly? I mean, other than this?"

He lifted his gaze to meet hers, and his smile was enigmatic. "Come now, love. Do you want all of my secrets in just one conversation?" He rose from the table and took her hand.

"Well, actually, you haven't told me any of your secrets. You've just been prying into mine."

When he kissed the back of her hand, a tremor tingled along her spine. "Best get going now, my dear. You have things to do and stories to leap."

She allowed him to get away with saying nothing about himself, she even allowed him to keep a hold of her hand as he lead her out of the restaurant—because it was nice, having someone hold her hand—but she didn't ignore the fact that he had pried about her personal life and had neglected to tell her his own.

She'd get to the bottom of this guy, one way or the other.

As he hailed a cab and told the cabbie to take them to Stratosphere—which was still a decent walk from where they were—she wondered what he was hiding from. Because he had to be hiding from something. No one would dress like the Mad Hatter and get involved with a random stranger just because.

He was either an out-of-work actor desperate for a gig, a guy with too much time on his hands, a crazy dude, or a man who was running from something and this was the only way he knew how to survive, a man playing a part in order to cope.

A man much like her.

Chapter Five

Alyssa thought she might have a panic attack. She'd already been feeling weird all day with the tight chest and the choking sensation, not to mention the overwhelming disorientation. Now, she just felt like she was going to run screaming from the building until she reached somewhere nice and quiet that was on firm, level ground.

She'd been okay in the lobby of the Stratosphere, had purchased her ticket for the stupid ride with no issue. Had even had her worst suspicions confirmed by a man in a suit that was stationed by the ticket booth who apparently worked for Gwenna. She was indeed supposed to do this fool's errand. Cool.

Hat-man was unusually silent as she twisted her fingers in front of her on their infinitely long ride in the elevator. All she could hear was her own heart thundering in her head like it was ticking down to her imminent doom. She was still doing relatively okay until she heard the *ding*. At that moment, her heart decided to wedge itself into her throat, thus blocking off her ability to breathe.

The elevator doors opened, and Hat-man strolled out. She squished herself back into the corner, drawing a confused expression from the elevator operator.

Hat-man turned back around upon realizing that she was not next to him. He frowned for a second, then reached back into the elevator and snatched her wrist. He yanked her out, drawing a squeak from her. The elevator doors closing behind her may as well have been the lid of her coffin.

She was immediately faced with the observation deck, which granted her a terrifying view of the entirety of Las Vegas and probably parts of Arizona. She dragged in a wheezing breath and grasped blindly at Hat-man's sleeve until she had enough balled up in her fist to squeeze.

"It's alright, love. You're not going to be able to fall out of the observation deck." He pried her fingers off of his sleeve and went to the window. He knocked on it. "See, very thick glass."

She shook her head, grabbed his sleeve again, then looked around wildly until her eyes fell upon a lounge area off to her left. She vaulted toward it, ordered a shot of tequila, asked for another one, and downed that one too—all before Hat-man caught up to her.

"Wow...alright, so in suggesting you have a drink to calm your nerves, I created a monster. Noted."

She stared at him blankly, then ordered another shot. After she downed that one, Hat-man raised an eyebrow and turned her gently away from the bar.

"Okay, love. Enough of that for now, hm?"

She shook her head frantically.

"Look, you being annihilated is not going to make things any better. You'll probably end up just getting the spins, which will be a whole other can of worms." He guided her away from the bar after tossing a couple of bills at the bartender. She wanted to tell him that wasn't necessary, but her voice was stuck.

He guided her toward the entry for the SkyJump, and she dug in her heels in terror.

"It's okay, I promise," Hat-man tried to soothe. "They put you in a harness and catch you at the bottom. It's perfectly safe."

"No!" she cried, wheeling out of his hold. "Nononononono. It's not happening." She couldn't even deal with the view through the glass. How was she supposed to be able to jump off the building and sail through the air? "I can't do this. I really can't."

"It's alright," he crooned as he continued to drag her. "It'll be fine. I promise. I've done this before."

"Screw you doing this before!" she shrieked. "Screw this entire thing!" She yanked her arm out of his grasp and staggered back. "You don't tell me what to do! *I* tell me what to do!" Her breath was shallow, and her vision felt off-kilter, like she was falling already. She put her head in her hands and tried to remember how to take in air.

"Oh, so that's still your attitude then," Hat-man snapped.

She glanced up at him, momentarily distracted by his clipped tone.

His eyes narrowed and he approached her, slow and languid, like some kind of jungle cat. "And are you always so controlling? Only doing what *you* want to do?"

She frowned, and her out of control vision steadied so that she could level a scowl at him. "Excuse me?"

"Well, it seems perfectly apparent that, while I've been with you, you are only interested in doing the things that are going to benefit *you*. If that's how you behave, no wonder your husband isn't speaking to you."

His flip tone had her seeing red. She advanced toward him. "How dare you? You know nothing about—"

"All you've been saying since I met you is this job, this job, *this job,*" he retorted. "Obviously, it's not that important to you if you don't even have the balls to accomplish task number two."

"What—I—" She opened her mouth and closed it, annoyed that she couldn't form a response and annoyed at his accusation. She chose to ignore her flustered feelings and just focus on her anger. "This job *is* important to me," she spat. "But that doesn't mean I can just wave a magic wand and make my fear of heights go away, you moron." She put her hands on her hips and raised her chin in a way she used to daunt her co-workers. She'd seen Gwenna do the same time and time again, and it always produced results.

Instead of making light of her words, as she expected him to do, he rolled his eyes. Her posturing had next to no effect on him. "Yeah, that seems like you. Do you always resort to bullying and name-calling when someone points out something you don't like? Better to deny the truth than face it, hm?"

His words shot through her like armor-piercing bullets, and they all landed directly into her heart. It hurt because she recognized the reality of what he was saying, and because of that, it really pissed her off. "Screw you!" she screeched. "You don't know me! Who are you? *Nobody*!" She advanced toward him, hoping to intimidate him by invading his personal space.

He apparently wasn't someone who intimidated easily,

because he matched her until they were almost nose to nose. "Oh, I don't know you? See if this scenario rings a bell. You go to work at the ass-crack of dawn, before your husband even wakes up. You run to your cubicle—because you are definitely not high enough on the food chain to have your own office—where you spend all day like a good little worker bee, saying 'yes ma'am,' and 'no ma'am,' and doing whatever task any of the higher-ups command you to do. You never contradict them, never argue. You just say 'yes ma'am' all day long, hoping that this day will be different than yesterday. 'Today someone is going to recognize my talent!' But what happens? The end of the day comes, and as you're preparing to go home, your boss tells you she needs you to work overtime. And you do it because you think, '*This* is my chance!' But then you finish your assigned task; no one gives you praise, no one thanks you even, and all of your butt-kissing, ignoring your husband's calls and texts on lunch break, bore no results. *No one cares about you.*"

He whispered the last part. Alyssa cringed, wanting to escape this barrage of truth.

Well, he hit the nail on the head.

"You go home to a dark house, where your husband has already gone to bed because he was *sick* of waiting up for you, *sick* of being a second-class citizen, and you eat some sad leftovers or some TV dinner monstrosity because you don't even care enough to make a decent meal for yourself. Then you go to bed, to repeat the same cycle all over the next day. Your house is a place to sleep, not a home. The man you married is a person who keeps that place to sleep for you, not a partner. You barely even know what is going on with him because you spend so much time absorbed in your own drama. You exist as two completely separate people. That's a couple of roommates, not a marriage. At the end of the day, what do you have, love? *Nothing.*"

As Alyssa processed his painful words, she realized she had tears hovering on her eyelashes. That made her even angrier. But as she tried to fight back, her response lacked the vehemence she was going for.

She pointed her finger at him and tried to blink her tears away. "Who are you to assume *anything* about my marriage?"

"Who am I?" If possible, he got even closer to her face.

"Who am I? I'm the one person not afraid to tell you the truth, *love*, which everyone else in your life is apparently terrified to do. Either that or maybe you just don't want to hear them. You live your life under the pretense of living it for everyone else, but really, you're just living it for yourself. Why? What do you have to prove?"

"I have to prove I'm worth something!" she shouted.

Never gonna happen. You can't see anything *through. You always run away*. Her own voice in her mind, once again speaking realities she would rather ignore.

"Worth something to whom?"

"That's my business!" she hissed, infuriated and bothered by this entire conversation, as well as by the taunting voice inside her own head. "What I choose to do and why I do it is *my* issue!"

Yeah, your issue all right. Except you're always trying to find a scapegoat so you don't have to take responsibility for that.

"Who is it?" he prodded. "Who are you trying to prove yourself to?"

"Tucker!" she cried, breaking under the pressure of his verbal assault. "I have to prove to him that I was right about this, that he is unreasonable! That we have to have *jobs*, not hobbies! That I was doing this for *us*! That all of this wasn't for nothing! That we can have a *life*, not just some weird Bohemian existence!"

"And do you want this job that badly?" For the first time, his voice actually rose in ferocity. "No matter what the cost?"

"Yes!"

"Then friggin' *fight* for it! You want it so badly, yet you are willing to throw it away because of some petty fear? Do you know how to fight for *anything*? Is there anything that you would go to lengths for? Throw away your own selfishness for?"

"I'm not selfish!" she cried, but her voice wavered and her chin trembled.

"Aren't you? You won't fight for anything—your husband, your job...all these things you claim are important to you. Yet here you are, whining about doing the SkyJump. You say you are hungry for something, yet when it threatens you, you decide to throw it away. If that's how you function, I'm not surprised that your husband wants nothing to do with you."

Something exploded inside of Alyssa like a powder keg, and she stabbed her finger into Hat-man's chest. "You think I don't know how to fight for anything? You think nothing matters to me?"

He shrugged flippantly.

"Watch me," she growled. She turned on her heel and strode toward the entrance to the SkyJump. She didn't think about the height, didn't think about the drop, didn't think about anything other than proving the obnoxious man in the stupid hat wrong.

Because he had to be wrong. She wasn't selfish. She wasn't.

She barely felt the man strapping her into her harness.

She had to prove them wrong, all of them. She wasn't selfish; she was being responsible. She had to prove to Tucker that *he* was wrong.

Why is he the one who's wrong? He's happy. What are you? A disaster.

"Are you ready, miss?"

She stared straight ahead and thought of Tucker, of the light in his beautiful blue eyes that had never died. Her eyes had lost that light a long time ago. Now, when she looked in the mirror, she only saw fatigue and dark circles.

"Miss?"

But that would change when she landed this job. She would be calling a lot of the shots. She wouldn't be an errand girl anymore, jumping through hoops all the time. She would finally be able to do something with her life, her dreams. She could get her life back together. All of this would be worth it then.

"Miss?"

Tucker would see. She hadn't abandoned their dreams together; she was making it possible for them to live their dreams. He would be able to act and not have to wait tables anymore. She could be the breadwinner, and in the process, she would be able to live her dreams as a designer. That was how it had to be. It was the only conclusion that made sense. She had been sacrificing all this time so that they could finally reach the goals they had set!

Tucker achieved his goals long ago. You ditched yours

because you got discouraged. He's doing what he loves, and he's good at it. He's even working two nights a week as a sous chef for a prestigious restaurant. When he never even went to culinary school. He had the drive. He had the ambition. The only thing you're good at doing is blaming everyone else.

"Miss!"

"Just do it. Get it over with," she muttered.

"Um....well, you have to jump. It's not like I'm going to push you."

Alyssa glanced at the young man, then down at all the rigging he had strapped her into. She looked over at the platform she had to jump from, and instead of feeling terrified like she expected, she just felt numb. The war in her own mind switched off and she thought if she jumped, at least she wouldn't have to think for a couple of seconds. At the moment, that seemed like heaven...not thinking...not feeling anything.

She turned and leapt.

Without any thought. Without any fear.

She just...did.

As the wind sailed past her face and body, tears leaked out of her eyes and she thought, *This is what dying feels like.* Also, *This is what flying feels like.*

She wanted to fly. She didn't want to be confined anymore, squashed anymore, ignored anymore. For years she had struggled to make her dreams work, and they never had.

A vision of her parents flashed through her mind. Yelling...there had been a lot of yelling. She had told them she was marrying Tucker. As upper middle-class with a strict view on higher education, all they had seen was a gypsy eccentric with no ambition. They had told her that their daughter was meant for more than that, and if she married him, they would never speak to her again.

They hadn't.

All these years. Not one word.

Tucker had graduated college, he was insanely intelligent, but they had never seen his focus; they had never seen his talent. They had never seen beyond his free spirit.

Maybe if she got this job, they would see. They would see

she had made something of herself, see that Tucker hadn't dragged her down.

Is that what you think he's done? Dragged you down? He's the one actually doing what he said he would do. What are you *doing?*

Suddenly, the air whipping by her face died down and her body slowed in its plummet. Alyssa barely registered that her feet had touched the ground. The employees were unlatching her while she just stood there, comatose, reliving things she had never had the guts to face.

Somewhere in her consciousness, she saw the confused exchange of glances between the two men helping her out of her harness.

"Uh...ma'am? You can go now..."

She turned her attention to him slowly and nodded almost imperceptibly. "H-How do I get back to the observation deck?"

They directed her, and she wandered the way they instructed, feeling disconnected, like a zombie—her body was moving, but she was only slightly aware of what was happening.

As she reached the seating area closest to where the SkyJump entrance was, she wasn't surprised to see Hat-Man sitting there. In some deep and odd part of her, she had known he would wait for her. Tears spewed out of her eyes and ran down her cheeks ridiculously fast as she approached. He caught sight of her; she saw his bewildered and concerned expression seconds before she collapsed onto a chair, sobbing.

"It's me!" she cried.

He was at her side instantly and had his arm around her. "What is?"

"Who I need to prove myself to. It isn't Tucker. I'm full of crap. It's always been me." She put her head in her hands and let loose years' worth of tears. "My family always rode me so hard; I always had to be perfect. The perfect student, the perfect lady, the perfect daughter, the perfect *everything!* Nothing was ever good enough. I didn't want to be perfect. I wanted to be *me!* Tucker didn't need me to be perfect. Tucker loved me for who I was inside. He saw some kind of value in me." She wiped at her eyes and sobbed again softly while her heart splintered quietly in her chest. She shook her head. "My family disowned me after I married Tucker. They didn't think he was good enough for me. I wanted to show them, show them all...but..." She drew in a shuddering breath and felt Hat-man's hand caress ever so gently across her shoulders in soothing circles.

"But?" he encouraged.

"I could never finish anything, never see anything through. I could never stick with it like Tucker could. *I* was the one with no focus, not him. I would get frustrated because my dreams weren't producing results. I *did* get frustrated. We were barely eating!" She let out another muffled sob. "The day I got hired at the magazine, I had an interview with two other people before I got to Gwenna—she insists on having the final say on all employees hired, even the mail room people and the janitors. When I had my final interview with her, she told me I had been working too long in the wrong field, and that my ideas, my vision, had finally found a home." She shook her head slowly. "I wanted so badly to believe that someone, *anyone*, could believe in *me*, that I just..."

"Lost yourself."

Alyssa let out a sigh and nodded slowly. "When I started getting better paychecks, when we were able to move into a better apartment, I felt like I was finally accomplishing something."

"It is easy to be distracted by things, but they can become addictions. It seems to me that the only person who needs to believe in yourself in you."

She sniffed and sat there for a few moments, staring down at the black vinyl seat. Then she turned her attention to the view from the observation window—Las Vegas in all its glory splayed out in front of her like a postcard. The sun was beginning to set, and the lights were starting to come on. The city was slowly morphing from a busy metropolis to the nightlife capital of the world right in front of her eyes. Along the horizon line, the sky glowed a dusky rose color. It was beautiful, and Alyssa briefly wondered what she would find if she followed that sunset. What was out there that she was missing?

"Did you do that on purpose?" she murmured absently.

"Did I do what on purpose?"

"All those things you said. Did you provoke me because you knew it would get me to jump?"

"It worked, didn't it?"

She turned her attention back to the stranger sitting next to her. "Why? Why me? Why the interest? Do you just sit in that coffee shop every day waiting for someone to walk in who you can attach yourself to?"

"No, usually I sit in that coffee shop every day and harass the staff because it amuses me. Today was different."

"How so?"

He shifted slightly so he could look her in the eye. "Despite the calm, poised exterior you were attempting to present, you looked like someone who had just been dropped into a different world, like you had no idea where you were or what you were doing...like you were lost. I know what it feels like to be lost." He shrugged. "Something about you made it so that I just couldn't walk away."

She gazed into his different colored eyes and wanted to touch his face, maybe to see if he was real, maybe to see if he would put his arms around her again. She never opened herself up to strangers, ever, but then she didn't feel like her normal self anymore. She felt exposed, confused, and like he was suddenly the only person in the world who understood anything about her.

"Something else happened when I jumped," she admitted. "Something kind of scary."

He gave her a quizzical expression.

"I wasn't afraid. It was okay that I was plummeting to my death...because I didn't have to worry about anything for a while. I didn't have to think or feel. I didn't care if my rigging failed and I went splat, just so long as I could keep feeling nothing." She shook her head and felt tears threaten again. "That is *not* me." One tear fell, and he reached up with gentle fingers to catch it. Alyssa closed her eyes at his touch, as it sent jolts of electricity tingling through her body. She knew it was wrong to have such a strong reaction to another man, but deep inside, it didn't feel wrong at all. It—he—felt...like home.

It made no more sense than anything else had thus far. She tried to summon guilt, but she couldn't. She tried to find the strength to pull away, but it was gone. She was tired of fighting everything anyway.

"It seems to me that you had a great floodgate of epiphanies burst open while you were flying stories upon stories down to the ground," he said. "Seems also as if you have been holding a lot of that in for some time, am I right?"

She nodded.

"Then it's not all that strange to want to feel nothing after having an onslaught of emotion like that. Don't dwell on it, love. Just move forward from here."

"I don't even know which direction forward is," she grumbled, averting her gaze downward. "Nothing feels like it makes sense anymore. This job feels like it has been a waste of my time. I feel like I've been lying to myself for...ever, and I'm pretty sure Tucker is done with me. Not that I blame him." Her heart twisted.

"Well, I'm not done with you."

His velvet voice caressed over her in a way that made warm shivers cascade across her skin. She looked up into his face; his eyes captured her with the genuine gentleness they reflected. His soft smile crumbled away every last remnant of anything normal she thought she knew. "Who are you?" she whispered.

The mirth came back into his expression almost immediately. "Maybe I'm the Jacob Marley to your Scrooge McDuck... Wait...no."

She raised her eyebrows. "Are you saying you're a creepy ghost come to show me the error of my ways? Because that wouldn't surprise me at this point. And yeah, you're getting your literature mixed up with cartoons now, friend." He chuckled, and some of her previous sorrow slipped away. "Seriously, though, what is your name? I have been calling you Hat-man to myself this entire time, and I feel like we should move past it."

"Hat-man, hm?" He sat back and regarded her for a moment. "Well, what do you think my name is?"

She narrowed her eyes at him. "I wish it was something totally boring like Joe or Bill."

"Well, now, that would be no fun at all. I would much rather be named something like Cornelius. That's a good name, don't you think?"

She folded her arms and stared him down. "*Is* your name Cornelius?"

He sighed in an overly dramatic fashion. "No, but I kind of always wished it was." He stood suddenly, whipped off his hat, and bowed theatrically...again. He grinned up at her with enough mischief that she considered just calling him Loki, then he said, "I'm afraid, love, that the only name I can leave you with is my own. Drake Manhattan at your service."

She blinked at him. "Drake Manhattan. That's your *name*? Drake is *my* last name!"

"It is, eh? Coincidence or serendipity? You make the call. Most of my friends just call me Manhattan. It's also my favorite cocktail, just FYI." He winked at her and a few strands of his wavy, golden hair fell roguishly into his face.

"So instead of calling you Hat-Man, I'm calling you Man-*Hat*tan. Perfect." She rolled her eyes and stood with a sigh. "I need to get out of here. I wasted enough time having an emotional meltdown. I'm even more behind than I already was."

"You're going to finish the interview then?"

She turned back to him with a slight frown. There was a note of something in his voice, something...sad? "I have to," she said. "For me. I need to know I saw something through."

A strange expression mixed with both pride and sorrow crossed his features ever so briefly before his breathtaking grin resurfaced. He stepped forward and offered his arm. "In that case then, love, let us move on."

"You're coming with me?" She couldn't hide either her surprise or her delight.

"Have to see how it ends now, don't I? I'm too far invested."

Alyssa smiled, took his arm, and for the first time in longer than she could recall, she didn't feel as if she was embarking on an arduous task like she had begun to feel her life was.

She felt like she was going on an adventure.

Chapter Six

"'Are you elite enough to go where others can't? Do you *shine* bright enough?' What the crap does that mean? And really, what is the point of these stupid riddles? Why not just have a nice, normal interview?" Alyssa all but flung the piece of paper down to the ground. Feeling aggravated, she pushed an errant strand of hair out of her face. She didn't like games, yet this entire interview was just that, and it was getting on her nerves.

Manhattan picked up the paper she had discarded. "Glad to see your surliness returning, love." He gave her a sidelong smirk as they hoofed it back up the Strip, going nowhere in particular.

Alyssa scowled. "I'm just saying. This is beyond ridiculous. Who wants to see their potential employees run around like rats in a maze?"

"Aren't all employees rats in a maze?"

She fumed silently. Point freaking taken.

"I imagine this boss of yours figures if you want the position bad enough, you'll go to any length. It may be ridiculous, but you can't deny it shows something about a person and their tenacity. Also, each clue does reveal a specific skill."

"It's still stupid. And where are we even going?" Alyssa snorted.

Manhattan glanced at her. "How should I know? Aren't you supposed to figure out the clue?"

She turned around to smack him in the arm. "Aren't *you* the one who said he was helping me?"

He folded his arms. "Aren't *you* the one who told me it was against the rules?"

Alyssa sighed and rolled her eyes. "Touché."

He grinned.

Just then, Alyssa glanced over Manhattan's shoulder as a white-haired woman came barreling full tilt out of a random liquor store with a 5-Hour Energy fused to her lips. She flailed her arms wildly then jumped into the cab that skidded to a stop curbside.

"Hurry!" she shouted as she jumped inside. "I'm running late!"

Alyssa's eyes bulged. "It's Lindy!" she practically screeched.

"It's who—whoa! What are you doing?"

Alyssa ignored Manhattan's slightly panicked tone as she jumped right out in front of the next cab. She didn't give much of a choice, so the driver stopped to keep from hitting her. Alyssa motioned Manhattan over then she jumped inside. "Follow that cab! I'll pay you double!" she shouted, stabbing her finger in the direction of the one Lindy had just taken.

"Good lord," Manhattan muttered as he strapped on his seatbelt just before the cab peeled out. "I guess I shouldn't question your desire to get the job done any longer. That drop off the Stratosphere really did something to you."

She arched an eyebrow at him. "What's wrong, Hat-man? Can't deal with a little bit of daring-do?"

"Daring-do? Is that what you call it? Because I call it playing chicken with a moving vehicle."

"*You* call it? *You* weren't doing anything. I did it. If it was gonna run anyone over, it would have been me."

"I know," he stated matter-of-factly. The look he gave her—stoic, pointed, devoid of all playfulness, with concern mirrored in his green depths instead—made a shiver go up her spine and her heart flutter.

She averted her gaze and cleared her throat, not knowing what to do with his concern for her safety. It was best to focus on the task at hand. Manhattan made her feel far too much.

They weaved through traffic and off the beaten path, a few blocks away from the actual Vegas strip. They finally pulled up in front of a red brick building with a flashing blue-green neon sign that said *Shine*.

"Shine," Manhattan muttered. "Do you 'shine' bright

enough? Makes sense. I don't know why I didn't make the connection."

Alyssa gave him a questioning look.

"Shine is one of the most popular and swanky nightclubs in Vegas," he supplied.

She frowned. "Well, I'm drawing a blank as to what the actual challenge is, and Lindy is nowhere to be seen. How is that possible? We followed her!"

Manhattan shrugged. "Maybe she figured out something we didn't."

"Or maybe we find out once we are inside." She threw some money over the seat at the driver. "Thanks," she shouted, then leapt out of the cab.

Alyssa strode up to the large, sausage-like island of a bouncer, who was smoking a cigar. She cleared her throat because he looked like part of the Italian mob, and she needed a moment to collect herself. As she approached, she threw her shoulders back and raised her chin in an authoritative fashion, but before she could even open her mouth, the bouncer held his hand out to stop her.

Alyssa came to a halt right as Manhattan caught up to her. The bouncer took a large drag and demanded, "Who are you?"

The cigar smoke encircled her like a cloud and she coughed, waving it away with her hand. "I'm Alyssa Drake. I'm here for the next portion of my interview." She brandished the slip of paper with the riddle on it like a prize.

The bouncer didn't even bother to look at it, just puffed another cloud of smoke at her and said, "Club doesn't open till nine. Fifty dollars entry." He gave her a once-over and sneered. "And we have a dress code."

Alyssa blinked. "No, wait. You don't understand—"

"Oh don't I?" The Titanic mob man's demeanor turned suddenly threatening. With his bald head and gravelly voice, he reminded her of Jason Statham on steroids. She retreated a few steps, and Manhattan was suddenly in front of her, shielding her.

"Look, lady, who are you?" the bouncer asked again.

"I-I just told you. I'm Alyssa Drake. I'm here for the job interview with Gwenna Vartz. I—"

"Blah, blah, blah. I don't care. You're not on the list? Fifty bucks entry. Club. Doesn't. Open. Till. Nine." He blew another puff of smoke directly at her.

Alyssa opened her mouth to argue more, but only inhaled his second-hand smoke and started to cough. Manhattan corralled her. "Look, love, that barge of a man isn't moving any time soon. Why don't you read the clue again? Maybe we missed something."

She looked over it, mumbled it to herself, but nothing was making any kind of sense. She was tired, and flustered, and growing weary of this. "I don't freaking know!" she finally spat, flinging the clue not necessarily *at* Manhattan, but in his general direction.

He caught it as it fluttered up against his chest. He started to read over it when Alyssa caught movement out of the corner of her eye. She glanced back over to the bouncer and saw a woman with hair black as night, looking like some sort of Hollywood actress on the red carpet, swagger up to the entrance. The bouncer never even looked at his coveted list, never interrogated, or even spoke to her. He simply lifted the hook on the rope barrier and let her in.

Alyssa's brain felt like it was moving like a herd of turtles through quicksand, but she slowly started to put the pieces together. She glanced down at her own attire. Business-casual at its best. And her hair was probably all over the place from flying through the air on the SkyJump. Her makeup was no doubt half off, and she imagined she looked like a tourist who was lost and out of her element. Not to mention, she probably didn't smell the best due to all of the running, nervous sweating, near panic attack, and emotional breakdown.

She reached out and snatched Manhattan's wrist. He raised a questioning eyebrow at her. "Read that clue again," she said. "Out loud." She glanced back at the bouncer. He looked around discreetly, as if to check if anyone was watching him, then reached into his coat pocket and pulled out a flask. Drinking on the job. Classy.

"'Are you elite enough to go where others can't? Do you shine bright enough?'" Manhattan read.

"That's it!" she cried. "I need to be able to get into that club without being on the list!"

He mused on it for a second, then nodded slightly. "Makes sense."

"And look at me! I look like I've...like I've..."

"Taken a trip down the rabbit hole?"

"Exactly," she said dryly.

"All right, well, that can be remedied. What time is it?"

She pulled her phone out of her pocket. "Almost seven-thirty."

"Perfect. We have time to go shopping, and I know a wonderful place for dinner. You did say you needed to stop at eight for dinner break, yes?"

She nodded. "And that mushroom salad did nothing for me. I'm gonna cannibalize someone soon."

His mischievous grin was brighter than the club's neon sign. He offered her his arm. "Will you do me the pleasure?"

She stifled the smile that wanted to surface. "Of cannibalizing you?"

The way he arched his eyebrow, slow and contemplative, made her regret her attempt at wittiness.

"That depends on *how* you mean that *exactly*..."

Her face burned like it had never burned before, and she grabbed his arm with force. "Come on, let's go," she grumbled, trying to ignore the way his chuckle heated her blood.

The Venetian ended up being the place closest to them with shops still open. It was the first bit of luck Alyssa had managed to stumble into all day. She hurried as much as she was able, trying on cocktail dress after cocktail dress at an insane pace. Nothing fit right, and she felt ridiculous. She wasn't a party girl. She was a professional. And underneath that, she was an artist...of sorts. She knew she needed to find something upscale enough to look like she frequented high-end clubs, but slutty enough to get waved on through without a second glance.

She had narrowed it down to two slightly skimpy dresses as eight approached. One was emerald green with just enough sparkle to warrant some attention, but not so much that she looked like an eighties prom victim. It was strapless with a sweetheart neckline and a plunging décolletage, and there was no way she would be able to wear a bra with it. Thank goodness she only had B-cups. She may be chafed by the end of the night, but at least she wouldn't be falling out, or have one boob sorta in place while the other took a field trip underneath her armpit. The dress was short, about three inches above her knees, but with the right kind of stilettos, she knew she had the legs to pull it off.

The other dress was a little bit longer and cobalt blue with a black lace overlay. It looked a tiny bit goth and edgy, and the back plunged almost to her butt crack. She wouldn't be able to wear a bra with this one either, but she had always thought she had a very nice back...as far as backs went.

She debated for a while, tried them both on numerous times, then finally just went with her gut—for two reasons. Her intuition was pulling her strongly toward one garment. And her gut was growling like a lion in the jungle. She was freakin' hungry. She didn't want to play dress up anymore. She wanted to eat. She could worry about all the details of her party-goer getup after she had some sustenance in her belly.

She made her rather expensive purchase—thank goodness for her MasterCard—and met Manhattan outside of the shop.

"Did you find something?" he queried.

"Feed me," was her only response.

"Yes, ma'am," he replied with a mock salute. He offered his arm again in that way that he did, and she took it, letting him guide her to an upscale, but casual enough Italian restaurant.

Alyssa immediately descended on the bread basket like a vulture with a fresh kill, then told Manhattan to order her whatever he knew was good while she checked her phone. Nothing. Her heart fell. She had really done it this time. She had murdered her marriage. Tucker had never ignored her texts before, no matter how angry they had been at one another. She felt like the bottom dropped out of what was left of her world, and a cold, heavy ache settled into her chest cavity.

She put her phone back in her bag, then flopped it to the floor. She felt more exhausted than she ever had in her life. Her shoulders slumped and she sighed. She glanced up at Manhattan, who had just finished speaking to the waiter, and smiled softly. "Thank you," she murmured.

He glanced at her with faint surprise. "For what, my dear?"

She enjoyed the way terms of endearment rolled off his tongue in everyday speech, like he was from a different time period altogether. "For sticking with me through this stupid day. I had convinced myself I didn't need anybody." She shrugged. "Turns out maybe I did."

He smiled and reached across the table to cover her hand with his. "It is my supreme honor and pleasure, Alyssa."

It was the first time he had used her name instead of "love" or something else that sounded equally as British. It seemed more potent somehow, like he was saying something deeper than just his words. Her heart responded to it, even though her mind couldn't decipher his message.

"I take it your husband has not responded to you?" he inferred. He pulled his hand slowly away and their strange moment dissolved.

She shook her head and looked down. The tablecloth pattern swirled as she fought tears. "I ruined it, Manhattan. I really did." She glanced back up at him and wiped away a tear that succeeded in escaping. "I can feel it. I have to get this job now. I have sacrificed everything for it. Now it's all I have left."

"Tell me," he said gently. "What would you do if there were no limitations? Not financially or opportunity wise? If you could just do whatever you wanted, what would it be?"

"I'd be an interior designer," she replied without hesitation. "Or maybe even dabble in fashion design. Just something where I could display my own work, my own creations, and be recognized for them."

He frowned thoughtfully and folded his hands in front of him under his chin. "And how will this job help you accomplish those dreams?"

"Well, I'll be Senior Creative Director of the magazine. *Fashion and Design of the Modern Woman* has all of those things in it—fashion and interior design. It's intended to appeal to all elements of a 'woman's' interest."

She air-quoted "woman's," and Manhattan smirked at her sarcasm.

"If I am Senior Creative Director, I get to decide what goes in the magazine. I get to decide what is best, what will make the magazine sell more copies, how we can reach a larger audience. I will be able to use my artistic eye."

"Yes...but all that really comes down to is you deciding who else's designs get to make it into the magazine. You chauffeur around everyone else's ideas, their talents. When do you get to use yours?"

Alyssa was dumbfounded for a moment, because she hadn't really thought of it like that. "Well, if I was boss, I could incorporate my own designs."

"Could you?" He met her gaze pointedly. "Because it seems to me that your boss is still *the* boss. Her say would be the final say. When do you get to have your final say, Alyssa? When do you get to use *your* ideas?"

She stared at him, rattled. He was right. She would still just be a slave. Granted, a higher-up slave, but still a slave.

"You want to design," he continued. "Well, this is journalism. It's advertising, not design. You want to be the client Gwenna Vartz is after, not the one organizing everyone else's ideas. Can you say that this job would prove different than that for you?"

She couldn't, and she couldn't wrap her mind around the fact that she hadn't realized that until now. Despite Tucker trying to tell her so many times. Despite even Manhattan dropping clues. It hadn't made sense until right this moment. It just about crushed her, because this was really all she had left now. She had fought so hard for it...for nothing. Everything that had mattered so much to her was nothing more than dust.

Right when she feared she would lose it, the waiter brought their entrées. Hers was pasta Bolognese, served with a Caesar side salad and a glass of red wine. She blinked at it for a moment before she looked up at Manhattan. "This is my favorite," she murmured. "How in the world did you know that?"

His expression was soft, kind, understanding. He gave a small shrug. "It just seemed like the right thing to order."

What she wanted to do and what she did do were two entirely different things. What she wanted to do was dissolve into a pile of sobs until the mysterious man she shared company with put her back together. What she did do was stab a bite of pasta with her fork and raise it to her trembling lips. "I'm going to eat. I need to eat. No more heavy conversations right now, okay?"

He seemed to get the point, nodded silently, and the two of them shared a quiet, yet comfortable dinner.

Chapter Seven

Alyssa let out a long, slow breath as she looked herself over in the full-length bathroom mirror. She had managed to procure some makeup and other necessities from a 24-hour Walgreens, and had given herself a scrub down with some paper towels and the soap dispenser in the bathroom. She felt moderately better, smelled—she imagined—a lot better, and looked decent...maybe. She felt kind of silly, all dolled up in a club dress with her back and the upper half of her hiney hanging out and her boobs flopping around.

She had opted for the blue and black dress with a pair of silver, strappy, stiletto heels, and had done her hair up pompadour style in the front with the sides pinned back and the rest flowing freely down to her shoulders. Her eyes she had done with a smoky, black eye shadow, edgy enough to match the dress, and had polished the look with some bronzer on her cheeks and a dark red lipstick.

She'd never felt more stupid in her life, and wondered briefly if this was how Tucker felt when he went out on stage.

Deciding it was as good as she was going to get, Alyssa left the bathroom to find Manhattan.

He was there, as he always was, waiting for her.

As if he had sensed her presence, he turned toward her, and she was surprised to find that he had changed also. He still had on the red jeans, but now he wore a purple button-down shirt with a black paisley print, and his eye makeup had gone from green and blue to a black starburst around only one eye. And the eye that had been red was purple now.

"You changed," she stated as she neared him, wondering what kind of magical universe he had pulled the clothes and makeup from since she had never seen him with a bag.

He seemed stunned for a moment, and after his eyes had

looked their fill of her, they met hers. "Well, yes. You are not the only one who needed to don club attire. I couldn't go looking like I did. I looked insane."

Alyssa smirked.

"But you..." He shook his head and regarded her as if she was something treasured, something to be savored. "You, love...there are no words."

She stood silent for a moment, gazing at him. She felt like she was on the cusp of something much more important than this dumb interview. "I feel ridiculous," she stated.

He moved closer to her, and his fingers fluttered ever so slightly down her hair. "One such as you...should *never* feel ridiculous."

Her breath caught at the way his lips formed those words. Like they were precious. She desperately wanted to sample what those lips tasted like, because she had never known such passion in her life. It seemed like he lived his whole life that way, passionately. Had she ever been that way? She didn't know anymore. She had felt that way with Tucker, in the beginning, but that felt like it had all happened in a completely different life.

"'I knew who I was this morning, but I have changed a few times since then.'"

She frowned, and Manhattan turned the full power of his grin on her, as if he had read her thoughts. The line sounded familiar, like she knew it from somewhere else deep in the recesses of her memory. "Lewis Carrol again?"

He nodded. "It seemed to fit."

The corner of her mouth lifted slightly. Maybe he could read her mind. Maybe he was made of magic. Maybe he *was* the freaking Mad Hatter. She didn't care anymore. All she knew was that he was with her, and he was in her corner. Nothing else really mattered outside of that.

Words stirred in her mind and found their way to her lips. "'I can't go back to yesterday, because I was a different person then.'"

His eyes sparkled. "You know the story well?"

She gave a small shrug. "I have read a lot of literature in my time. I tend to remember a lot of quotes. Seems the more I am with you, the more I remember."

"Curioser and curiouser." He smirked.

She smiled, then moved forward impulsively and wrapped her arms around him in a hug. She heard him draw his breath in sharply and felt his arms twine around her as well, holding her close to him. She closed her eyes and reveled in his warmth. She didn't know when exactly it had happened, but at some point during this carnival ride of a day, this half-insane man had become the only real thing that made sense in her life.

His hand came up to entangle in her hair, and he tightened his embrace slightly, as if he didn't want to let her go. A wave of sadness and slight desperation came off of him; it twisted her heart as much as it confused her. She wanted to ask him what he was feeling, what was wrong, but it didn't seem like the right time. And she imagined he would deflect into humor and not tell her anyway.

She pulled back and searched his eyes, but found only warmth there. "Ready to do this thing?" she asked.

He turned and offered his arm. It was the only invitation she needed.

There was a line outside of the club now. Fantastic. And Italian Jason Statham didn't look any friendlier than he had before. He was scrutinizing everyone that went through, and sent several people away regardless of the fact that they were willing to pay the entry fee.

"I have no idea how I am supposed to do this," Alyssa grumbled. "He is going to recognize me. Even if he doesn't recognize me, he is definitely going to recognize you."

"Go ahead and do your thing, love. I can find my own way in." He took her hand and pressed a kiss to the back of it.

Alyssa turned to argue, but he had already vanished. She looked around in bewilderment. It was like he had snapped his fingers and disappeared! What was he, a stinking genie? She chose not to dwell on it. Best not to at this point. She shook her head and tried to gather her wits. Okay, she had to act like she belonged at the club. She couldn't go scurrying up there like a frightened mouse. She needed to exude confidence and authority.

She needed to act like Gwenna.

"All right, let's get this over with," she muttered to herself. She raised herself taller, shook out her hair, and strode over with purpose. She went right to the front of the line, ignoring the people waiting to get in.

"Hey!" the skanky-looking woman at the front complained.

Alyssa shot her the best shut-up-you-peasant look she could manage, then reached for the hook on the rope barrier.

Jason Statham's beefy hand came down to grasp her wrist. "Who are you?" he growled.

She snatched her arm away from him and put her hand on her hip. "Who am *I*?" she spat. She looked him up and down with disdain. "Who are you, *little man*?" She took delight in the fact that his eyes flashed with anger. Especially since he towered over her five feet, seven inches.

He seemed to contemplate the situation for a moment before he said, "You on the list then?"

She let out a noise that sounded affronted, offended, and downright pretentious. "The list? Seriously? You honestly don't know who I am, Guido?"

His expression went from angry to slightly concerned, like he was wracking his brain trying to figure out who he had just insulted. He frowned. "Well, you do look a little familiar."

She jumped on that. "Of course, I do, you hulking moron! I'm at a VIP table here every time I'm in Las Vegas!"

"Uh...well, I'm sorry, but I still need your name so I can check you off the list."

She huffed and crossed her arms over her chest. "If you do not let me into this club right this instant, I will have your job, you drunken buffoon. Or did you think I *couldn't* smell the booze on your breath?"

His eyes widened slightly before he seemed to grow a foot taller in an attempt to intimidate her. It worked, but she didn't back down. "Watch who you're accusing, ma'am," he snarled.

Her eyes narrowed and she smirked, then managed to do the best—and only—pickpocketing she had ever done. She darted her hand into his suit coat and yanked the flask out. She waved it in front of him in arrogant triumph. "Watch who *you're* threatening."

He looked horrified then he gathered his composure,

stepped back, and unhooked the rope. She scowled, shoved the flask up against his chest, and marched inside like she owned the place.

Once she got past the door, she had to lean against the nearest wall because her legs felt like they were made of jelly and her heart was hammering against her ribcage like it wanted to escape.

"Job well done, love."

Alyssa screamed and jumped almost to the ceiling. "How did you get in here?" she cried at Manhattan. He opened his mouth, but she waved her hand at him and shook her head. "You know what? Never mind. I don't even want to know. I think I just pooped my pants."

He laughed and ran his hand down her bare back. She shivered. "You see?" he murmured. "When you put your mind to something, you *can* accomplish it, can't you?"

She wanted to wither. She was seriously *so done* with this. Stupidly, she felt tears gathering in her eyes. She was becoming completely unbalanced.

"Oh...no, no," Manhattan chided, taking hold of her shoulders. "Snap out of it, love."

She shook her head and wanted to bawl like a baby. "I just wanna get out of here," she half-sobbed. "Where is the guy I'm supposed to go to after this?" She scanned the room, and amidst the strobe lights and thumping music, found a man who looked completely out of his element. She zeroed in on him. "*That* guy!" she exclaimed. He was standing by the bar, looking awkward. She snatched Manhattan by the arm and dragged him behind her as she beelined toward the stranger. "Do you work for Gwenna Vartz?" she all but screamed.

The guy was slightly taken aback and took two steps away from Alyssa, then held up his hands. She must have looked as insane as she felt.

"Who are you?" he queried.

"Seriously?" she spat. "How many times do I have to answer that stupid question?" She was two seconds away from throwing a temper tantrum like a three-year-old. Wailing away on the ground with her fists and feet...the whole nine yards. "I'm Alyssa Drake! I'm here for this absurd interview! What is my next freaking clue?" She felt Manhattan's gentle caress over her hand, and she eased somewhat.

The kid looked scared. It gave her a modicum of satisfaction. "I-I'm sorry, but the next task has been compromised."

She frowned. "Compromised? What is this, the CIA? What does that even mean?"

"Something went wrong and...it's stalled. You're stuck here for the time being."

"Stuck here?" Her voice was getting progressively more screechy. "What do you mean stuck here?"

He shrunk back. The guy looked no more than freshly-turned twenty-one. Probably an intern. "I mean you can't advance with the interview yet. You made it in here, but if you did that, then you obviously don't have a wristband or anything, so you can't go back out again. You have to stay here until..." He gulped. "Until I tell you you're finished."

If daggers could have come out of her eyes, he would have been dead. "Until I'm *finished*?" she hissed.

"Yes...those are my instructions. I will let you know when you can proceed."

"And what am I supposed to do until then?"

He shrugged. "Dance? Have a drink with your...friend?" He gestured at Manhattan.

Alyssa stared at him long enough to make him squirm a bit, until Manhattan gently tugged on her arm and drew her away from the poor boy.

"What is the point of this?" she snapped as she rounded on Manhattan, her hair flying behind her. Any second now, her eye was gonna start twitching. She just knew it.

He took her by the shoulders and ran his fingers down her arms, soothing her.

Her irritation melted back into that vulnerable place she had been in moments ago, and she shook her head, her eyes burning again. "I'm tired," she murmured. "I just want to go home." A tiny sob escaped her throat. "If I even have a home anymore."

He immediately enveloped her in his arms, and all was right in her world. She buried her face against his shoulder and knotted her fingers in the fabric of his shirt until she managed to pull herself together. When she moved away and drew in a calming breath, the way he looked at her— gentle, understanding, so kind—was enough to almost make her lose it again. She felt like she didn't deserve his kindness, his help, anything he had offered her.

He took her face in his hands, and met her eyes with intensity. "You need a drink, love," he stated.

She snorted out a laugh, then nodded, relinquishing to this strange turn of events and surrendering to whatever it might lead to. She had been either uptight or an emotional wreck all day. She was exhausted. If she was being instructed to drink and dance while she was at this swanky club she had just bullied her way into, so be it.

Manhattan led her to the bar, where a scantily-clad woman with crazy cyber-punk hair was bartending. She flashed Manhattan a dazzling grin while she barely acknowledged Alyssa's existence. "What's your poison, sexy?" she purred.

Why Alyssa felt the overwhelming need to jump over the bar and tear the woman's eyes from her skull, she couldn't quite figure out. She tried to squash the bizarre impulse and chalk it up to stress.

"A Manhattan, please," he ordered, and Alyssa noticed that he did not address her as "love." She had figured it was just the way he spoke, but she realized that he had not called anyone but her that all day.

The woman leaned over the bar, showing off her ample cleavage, and reached for Manhattan's hat. "This is an interesting getup," she murmured, her voice all dark and sex-pot-like. "Are you the Mad Hatter then?" She removed his hat and placed it on top of her own head, adjusting it and tipping the brim like a trained model.

Alyssa almost lost her mind. She shoved her way in front of Manhattan, reached over the bar, yanked the hat off of the bartender's head, and placed it firmly on her own. "I'll have a dirty martini," she growled.

The woman arched an eyebrow and backed away, then proceeded to make their drinks.

Still seething, Alyssa turned to face Manhattan, who was leaning nonchalantly against the bar with an amused smirk on his lips. He slid his gaze over to her. "It's a nice look for you," he stated.

Alyssa's face turned hot as she realized how she had just behaved. What in the world was wrong with her? She was married, for crying out loud. Even if she didn't know for how long that would be a fact, she still was. Why was she jealous over a woman showing Manhattan some attention? After this whole thing was done, she would be back in L.A anyway. She would probably never see him again...

"You look better in it than she ever could." He had leaned close to her, and the low timbre of his voice reverberated throughout her entire body. He dropped a soft kiss to her shoulder; she closed her eyes. His lips may as well have been a branding iron for the way her skin burned.

She turned her head so she could look at him, and his eyes captured her. Something in them...she couldn't place what it was, but they held her entranced. When she looked into them, she felt like she never wanted to stare into another pair of eyes for as long as she lived.

What *was* her draw to him? Was it because he had stood by her? Or was it because those eyes she wanted to lose herself in saw straight through her? He didn't let her justify herself out of where she had ended up in her life. He boldly challenged it, and forced her to do the same. He made her face the skeletons in her closet she had always run from. And in doing so, he was making her realize she was nowhere near where or what she wanted to be.

Was that what she wanted? His guidance? Like some sort of bizarre circus escapee therapist?

Or was it more than that?

Maybe...

Maybe it was just that, for the first time in such a long time, she didn't feel alone.

"Drake Manhattan," she murmured.

"Yes, love?" His voice was just as hushed.

A strange calm came over her, and she didn't know why, but she suddenly knew everything was going to be all right. One way or another. She lifted his hat off of her head and gently placed it back on his. "I don't know why you took a chance on me. I don't know why you even care, but I want you to know that, despite everything...my witchy behavior, my freak outs, the really crappy way I treated you early on, I really appreciate everything you have done for me today. I don't know where you came from, and I don't know if I'll ever see you again after tonight, but you need to know...you made a difference." She shook her head. "I won't take it for granted, I promise." Emotion was clogging her throat, but she forced a smile. "You really are rather exceptional."

His eyes grew soft, warm, and he reached up to cup her cheek in the most tender of gestures she had ever experienced. "Live your life, Alyssa Drake," he whispered, his breath caressing her lips. "After all of this madness is done with, live your life for you and you alone. Your dreams, your passions, your love. If you do that, somewhere in the chaos, I will know it, and I will be smiling."

Her eyes fluttered closed and she leaned into him, wanting his breath, his warmth, his logic, his compassion, his magic...his madness within every fiber of her own being. If she could only live her life as he did, with such abandon, such boldness, such creative eccentricity.

Wasn't that what she had always wanted? When had it eluded her? Oh right, when she'd sold out because of frustration and turned into a total douchebag.

The noise of the club fell away as he leaned toward her, his lips scant inches from hers. She closed her eyes, aching, yearning for his kiss. No matter how wrong it seemed, it felt right...it felt like the piece she'd been missing. She needed this...

She needed him.

"Here are your drinks."

The magic of the moment was shattered by the bartender crashing their drinks down on the bar top. Alyssa blinked away the spellbound daze she was in and grasped her martini glass, noticing that the bartender was scowling at her.

Manhattan threw some bills up on the bar and turned back to Alyssa. He took a sip of his drink and grinned. "Dance with me," he murmured, his velvet voice an invitation she could never turn down.

Chapter Eight

On the dance floor, Alyssa lost herself. She was so tired of being proper all the time, of being professional and everything that entailed. She was sick of it. She wanted to be free. When was the last time she had been free? Geez, she didn't even know. She had spent so much of the last few years running and jumping for everyone, everyone other than anyone who mattered.

Running from herself, her past, her failures...everything.

She had been so despondent when she had applied to work at the magazine. Journalism had never really been on her to-do list, but she wasn't bad at it. At the time, Tucker had been between jobs, and she couldn't find work in her desired field to save her life. She had been desperate, and tired of slaving away for nothing. All she could hear were her parents' voices, telling her she was making a mistake, that Tucker would drag her down, that she was throwing away her education and her intelligence and would never amount to anything. She had started to feel more and more useless, not just secularly, but in her marriage, and to herself.

She hadn't told Tucker everything that had been going on inside her. She wasn't the best at communication, and she wasn't great at facing her problems either. She had been a pushover her whole life, being bull-nosed by her parents since she'd come out of the womb.

The only thing she had ever stuck up for had been Tucker. Because he had mattered that much to her.

Having Gwenna validate her had made her feel like she could finally do something with her life, make the voices of doubt in her head shut the hell up.

But here she was, three years later, still slaving away for nothing.

She went home exhausted, woke up exhausted, and had been living life as a zombie for longer than she wanted to think about. Dawn had made her wake up, made her realize what a shallow jerk she was becoming, and Manhattan had continued on with that wake-up call.

Maybe he *was* her Jacob Marley.

Who knew? Who cared?

All that mattered to her at this moment was that she was dancing. Dancing when for so long she had been stagnated. The throbbing pulse of the music resonated inside of her, and Manhattan's body against hers felt fantastic, perfect, like something she had been missing had clicked into place. He moved like the music—fluid, sensual, enticing.

She wrapped her arms around his neck and let the movements of his body lead her, take her away. In that moment, nothing and no one else existed. She was okay with that. She never wanted to face reality again.

"You should live the way you dance, love," he called over the thrum of the music.

She frowned inquisitively.

"Without restraint, with abandon, like this moment is all you have."

Part of that statement felt true, like this *was* the only moment she had. If she got this job, who would she be then? Not someone dancing the night away with a man wearing makeup and a hat. Did she want to give that up? She no longer knew. At the beginning of the day, if someone had told her this was where she would end up, she would never have believed it. She wouldn't have been caught dead dancing with someone like Manhattan. Now, all she knew was that being with him felt like the only place she needed to be.

Maybe it was the martini she had drank, or maybe it was the fact that she just didn't care anymore. About much. She wanted to feel something, *anything*, and he made her feel everything. That was enough for her.

That was all to her.

Acting on sheer impulse, and with little to no thought whatsoever, Alyssa grasped Manhattan behind the neck and pulled his lips to hers. He stiffened for a moment, as if in shock, then he melted against her and his arms came around her in a gentle embrace. His lips moved over hers, soft, teasing.

Alyssa felt her knees tremble, and she pressed up against him as close as she could, entangling her fingers in his blond hair at the nape of his neck.

He reached one hand up to cradle her jaw, then deepened the kiss.

Something inside of Alyssa detonated at the feeling of his tongue caressing hers. It was like every warped and scattered puzzle piece of her life fell into place. The music faded away, and nothing else mattered. She wanted to kiss him forever. It was like he was breathing life into her, keeping her soul alive. Her heart went supernova and sent fire burning through every single vein in her body.

She didn't want to pull away, but she needed to in order to breathe. His fingers knotted in her hair, keeping them connected, and he rested his forehead against hers. "I don't know how you expect me to go without that now," he murmured, as breathless as she was. "I amend my last statement. You shouldn't live how you dance. You should live how you kiss."

She smiled, and reached her fingers up to trace his lips. She felt like her heart was screaming something at her, leaping and cavorting in an effort to get her attention, but she had no idea what it was trying to say. She shook her head, subtle quivers running all throughout her as his eyes came up to lock on hers. "Why...why do you feel so familiar to me?"

She didn't know how he could hear her over the music, but he did, and his smile was enigmatic and sexy. He eased his lips back onto hers, and she savored his possession.

Out of nowhere, a terrible, raging siren of a sound blared through her ears, threatening to split her skull in two. She cried out and put her hands over her ears, doubling over as a wave of dizziness passed over her.

"Alyssa!"

Manhattan's voice sounded like it was coming from the other end of a tunnel, and as she thought that, she swore she could see said tunnel, forming and spinning out in front of her.

"Alyssa, what's wrong?" She was vaguely aware of his hands gripping onto her shoulders. "Alyssa!"

"What is that terrible noise?" she screamed. She felt like it was hammering inside of her head, and the dizziness got worse to the point that nothing felt real. She felt like she was being sucked into whatever vortex that awful sound was creating.

"No, no, no!" she heard Manhattan shout. "Not yet!" If she didn't know better, she would think he was afraid.

She felt like maybe she was moving, but she couldn't be sure because even the pressure of his hands on her was starting to fade into nothingness. "Manhattan," she whimpered. "Manhattan, help." But her voice was sucked into that dark tunnel, which was looming ever closer to her. Her body began to feel weightless, strange, like she was dissolving into nothing.

"No!" His voice sounded further away now. "Alyssa! Stay with me! I'm not nearly finished with you yet!"

The blaring noise finally ceased, and for a moment, Alyssa felt like she was floating, suspended between two different places. There was no sound, there was no movement. Just empty space as the particles of herself wandered around the entrance of the tunnel. She wasn't sure how long she drifted there, but slowly, she became aware of her own heartbeat again, of the breath she was dragging into her lungs. She heard muffled sounds she couldn't distinguish, and she concentrated on them.

There was a voice she recognized. She held onto that voice and tried to travel toward it.

"Alyssa! Please! Don't leave me yet." There was sorrow in the voice, an ache she didn't like. She struggled to get back to that voice, but her body wouldn't cooperate, wouldn't move.

Then, blackness.

Alyssa was walking across campus toward the parking lot, where her mother was waiting for her by the car. They always ate lunch together on Wednesdays. No doubt her mother's friends thought it was sweet, but Alyssa knew the real reason they went to lunch every week was so that her mom could pump her for information, grill her on dorm life, make sure she wasn't doing anything off-color, seeing any boys, joining any unsavory extracurricular activities, letting her studies slip, or basically any other thing her parents could come up with to ensure she never had a life. It got old; she was completely tired of it, and she wondered when her parents would give it a rest and realize she was a grown woman, not a child.

She hadn't told them that her major was going to be in interior design. As far as they were concerned, she was studying to be...who knew what? Something prestigious that they could brag about and ride on her coattails for. They would flip out if they knew she was studying practically all of the arts just because she wanted to.

"Well hello, my dear lady!"

Alyssa jumped back a step as a guy dressed in a black button-down shirt, a black pinstripe vest, and slacks to match suddenly descended in front of her.

She blinked in bewilderment and looked him over, more startled and confused than anything. His black shaggy hair was a disheveled mess that reminded her of Robert Smith from The Cure, and he had on enough eyeliner to make it seem like his light blue eyes were stabbing into her. She thought she recognized him from her poetry class, but the semester had just started, so she couldn't be sure.

She opened her mouth to say something, but she never got the words out.

"'Shall I compare thee to a summer's day? Thou art more lovely and more temperate.'" He gestured up to the sun as it beamed down on them, and then bowed low before her with a mischievous grin.

She arched an eyebrow and folded her arms over her chest. "Shakespeare's Eighteenth Sonnet. Really? How cliché. Can't you come up with anything better than that?"

He seemed slightly taken aback by her response, but his expression showed he was intrigued by the challenge. He straightened, thought for a moment, and then said, "'He stepped down, trying not to look long at her, as if she were the sun, yet he saw her, like the sun, even without looking.'"

Alyssa smirked. "Leo Tolstoy, Anna Karenina."

His smile broadened to a degree that it made her heart thump stupidly in her chest. He took a step closer to her, standing tall now, sure of himself. "'The power of a glance has been so much abused in love stories, that it has come to be disbelieved in. Few people dare now to say that two beings have fallen in love because they have looked at each other. Yet it is in this way that love begins, and in this way only.'"

She narrowed her eyes at him, playful, undaunted. "Vic-

tor Hugo, Les Miserables.*"*

He raised one dark eyebrow. "A woman who knows her literature. Be still my breath and my heart. 'You should be kissed and often, and by someone who knows how.'"

Alyssa felt her cheeks turn pink because of the way his hushed voice murmured the words down at her. She cleared her throat and looked away discreetly before she dared meet his penetrating eyes again. "Margaret Mitchell, Gone with the Wind.*"*

The boldness in his eyes, the ice they resembled when battling, melted into the most amazing liquid smoldering blue fire she had ever seen. His playful posturing relaxed, and he came to stand close to her, gazing down at her like he had never seen anything like her in his life. "'Well, now that we have seen each other, if you'll believe in me, I'll believe in you.'"

Alyssa lost herself in his eyes and never wanted to come back out. "I know that was Lewis Carroll...but I forget which book. Either Alice in Wonderland *or* Through the Looking Glass.*"*

His gaze traveled over her face like a reverent caress. "I fear I've fallen into a pit of love so deep and so vast that I may never find my way back out...nor do I want to."

She was sure her heart had never beat so fast in her life. She felt exhilarated by his presence, drawn to him inexplicably. It threw her off and made her feel self-conscious and unsure. She took an awkward step away and giggled shyly before throwing her shoulders back and meeting his gaze with false bravado. "Okay, you got me. What's that from?"

The step she took back, he made up for by advancing on her even closer than before. It wasn't imposing, his presence, just overwhelming, resonating...intoxicating. "Tucker Drake...right now...sophomore year."

She stared at him, surprised, touched, and so moved by his unconventional presence in her conventional world. She wanted to lean into him, breathe his essence in, sample a taste of his lips that were hovering so close to her own, drown in the ocean of his eyes.

"Alyssa! What are you doing? Come on!"

She jumped and looked over to where her mom was standing at the curb, waiting for her impatiently. All of her air

whooshed out of her and her face burned. "I-I have to go,"
she stammered. "I'm having lunch with my mom."

She tried to move past him, but he grabbed her wrist.
"Wait." He turned toward her, intent. "Come to the little theatre tomorrow after class."

"Why?" she questioned.

"Because that's where I am going to be, and I want you
everywhere that I am."

Her heart skipped a beat and she laughed breathlessly.
"What? You're insane. You don't even know me."

He stepped up to her again, towering over her, invading
her space in the best way. "No, but I want to," he all but
whispered. "I want to know every single part of you...in glorious detail."

If he kept talking to her, either her legs were going to
give out, or she was going to let him enfold her in his arms
and never leave his embrace again. No one had ever spoken
to her with such boldness, such confidence, such passion.

"Alyssa!"

Her mom's voice jarred her back to the present again, in
grating shrillness. "I have to go," she murmured.

"Please, say you'll meet me tomorrow." He held onto her
hand until she managed to slip her fingers from his grasp.

She bit her bottom lip and smiled bashfully, heading
across the lawn toward her mother.

"'Whatever our souls are made of, his and mine are the
same!'" he called after her.

She stopped and turned back toward him, smiling. "Emily
Brontë, Wuthering Heights."

In that moment, his grin captured her heart for all time.
"Please say you'll meet me tomorrow. Please, come back to
me!"

She laughed but didn't answer as she ran the rest of the
way to where her mother was waiting.

"Please, Alyssa, come back to me."

The scene began to dissolve, and her ears suddenly filled
with throbbing bass and techno music. She drew in a labored
breath; her eyelids fluttered open. She was seated on something, and she was leaning against a man's chest. His arms
were wrapped around her so tightly she almost felt like she
was suffocating. She could feel his heart thundering against

where her ear was pressed. She slowly raised her head and drew in a few shaky breaths. Her surroundings swam for just a second, but the feeling vanished quickly. She reached up and touched some wetness on her cheek, then brushed it away. She turned her gaze up into the concerned face of the man who was holding her. "Manhattan?" she squeaked.

He expelled a breath and his arms relaxed slightly. "You all but stopped my heart, love."

"What happened?" She brought a shaky hand up to her head and smoothed her hair self-consciously.

"I think you fainted."

She frowned. "What was that noise?"

His brows drew together slightly and he shook his head. "I didn't hear anything."

She chose not to tell him about reliving the first moment she had met Tucker. She couldn't even think about that right now. If she did, she would lose it enormously. "It was awful, like some screaming siren. And then it felt like I was being...sucked out of here...through a tunnel. That's the only way I can explain it. I...I heard your voice. You said not to go, that you weren't...finished with me yet." She looked back up at him. "What do you mean you're not finished?" Suddenly, Alyssa remembered what the intern had said to her when she had entered the club. "Finished," she murmured. "We'll let you know when you're...*finished.*" She grasped Manhattan's wrist. "That was the clue!"

He stared at her for a moment before he reached up to run his hand along the length of her hair. "Did you bump your head when you passed out, love?"

She swatted his hand away and sat up straighter. "No, listen to me. That kid said that something had gone wrong with the next task, and that he would let me know when I was *finished*. That means if I didn't figure out what he meant, if I just gave up, I would be eliminated from the interview process! *That* was the clue!"

Manhattan frowned. "But...why?"

"Uh...because...at the magazine, monkey wrenches get thrown into projects all the time, obstacles arise. Gwenna wants to know how well we handle those things. When we are put in a frustrating situation, will we just give up and go with it, or will we force our way around it, find an out no one can see? It makes perfect sense."

"Perfectly insane sense."

She raised her eyebrow at him. "Says you."

He smirked and averted his gaze, looking slightly unsure for the first time all day. "All due respect to your one-track mind, love, but I much preferred what we were doing before you decided to black out on me." He turned the power of his mysterious gaze and gorgeous grin on her, and Alyssa felt her cheeks redden.

She looked down at her lap. "Oh...I shouldn't have done that." Her heart twisted painfully and she shook her head, feeling embarrassed, guilty, and bothered that her blood still burned every time she thought about kissing him again.

"But you did."

He whispered it against her ear, a sensual purr, and shivers exploded all over her. She sucked in her breath and looked up into his eyes again. They caught her and held her prisoner. A thousand things rattled through her mind that she wanted to say. What came out was, "I have to get out of the club. Are you coming with me?"

The gentleness that resonated from his eyes almost devastated her. He ran his finger ever so lightly along her bottom lip. "Of course I am coming with you." He watched the path he traced along her mouth, then looked up at her again. "I will always go with you."

Her heart pinched again. She knew she needed to get out of there before she did something completely insane, like find a chapel and get double married to this man. She stood too quickly, and dizziness swamped her again. She staggered; Manhattan immediately stood and grasped her arms to steady her.

"Oh my gosh, what is wrong with me? Do you think that crazy bartender put something in my drink?"

He shrugged one shoulder in a lazy motion, then grinned wickedly at her. "If you were roofied, I will be a perfect gentleman, I promise. I will only take advantage of you once or twice... Three if you ask me nicely."

She smacked him halfheartedly on the chest, but was happy to get back to their playful banter. Although, a very wanton part of her wondered just how much of a reality his proposition would become if she let him have his way.

Before she could think about it any longer and either 1—incinerated from lust she couldn't seem to put a lid on, 2—passed out again, or 3—burst into tears for the hundredth time that day, she straightened her dress and headed for the main entrance of the club.

She was about to head out when the kid from before blocked her path. "I'm sorry, you can't leave," he stated.

She looked up at him in confusion. "I beg your pardon?"

"You can't leave, ma'am. You have to wait until—"

"I'm finished? Right, I get that, and it's not happening. Get out of my way, slick. I know this is part of the task."

He swallowed uncomfortably. "I'm sorry, but you can't leave the club."

Alyssa stared him down until he started to squirm. "You can't keep me here against my will. I'm pretty sure that's illegal. Besides, I know for a fact I could take you in a fight, kid."

He shuffled on his feet nervously. "Maybe you can take me, but I doubt you could take him." He pointed over his shoulder to the monstrous troll of a man standing at the exit.

"Good lord," Alyssa muttered. "Where did you get these people? The land of the giants?"

"The bouncer out front really works here. But that guy is stationed there specifically to not let applicants leave the club until Gwenna says."

Alyssa's faith in her puzzle solving skills wavered for a moment. Maybe they *were* supposed to just wait there. Maybe they were all supposed to be in one place for the last stage of the interview. But...if that was the case, why were Lindy and Susan nowhere to be seen? Something didn't jive.

She was reminded of a time when Gwenna's old assistant had been told by another employee that Gwenna had canceled an appointment. The assistant had cleared it from the schedule, never mentioned it to Gwenna, and Gwenna had lost the opportunity to have an exclusive interview with a very famous fashion designer. Needless to say, the assistant had been fired, the misinformed employee had been fired, and Gwenna had bellowed that anyone who acted on something that did not come directly from her lips would be put on the chopping block.

Alyssa wasn't stupid. She knew how this game was played. She flashed the intern the stink-eye and sidled up to him. "Nice try," she sneered.

She swore the kid started to sweat; he backed up a step. "You are more than welcome to finish early, if you like," he stammered. "I can tell Gwenna that you decided to go home."

"Don't. You. Dare." She punctuated each word with a stab to his chest with her finger. "I will *finish* this stupid game when *I* decide to finish. And I will play it by *my* rules." She spun on her heel and strode back through the club.

"You can be rather intimidating when you want, my dear," Manhattan said as he hurried to keep up with her. "I think that boy needs to go change his drawers. Also, I give you props for tenacity in this situation."

"It's not even about the job anymore," she spat. "It's about being told what I can and can't do. I've been someone's patsy for far too long, and I'm realizing I am very, *very* sick of it."

She saw him smirk out of the corner of her eye. "Right, and where are we going then?"

"I'm finding a way out of here if I have to crawl through a freaking air duct."

"Oooh, *Mission:Impossible* style. I like it. I must say, your passion is turning me on, love."

A slow, sly smile spread across her lips and she gave him a sidelong glance. "It's kind of turning me on too. Feeling something." His approving grin sent waves of warmth over her. She headed toward the back of the club, insistent on completing this weird gauntlet if it killed her.

Chapter Nine

Alyssa managed to find the corridor to what she imagined was the dressing room for the performers she had seen throughout the night putting on acrobatic shows for the entertainment of the club-goers. She figured, she had been in enough theatres in her day with Tucker, and those *always* had a back door for the actors. She didn't imagine this place would be much different.

She bulldozed her way into the back corridor, finding several different doors, none of which were labeled. One was a bathroom. That was hardly helpful. One was a janitor's closet. The third door she opened was a dressing room, and she burst inside to see a woman frantically unstitching white roses on a gown. When the woman didn't even acknowledge her presence, Alyssa headed through another corridor she spotted.

"There's a guard back there."

Alyssa stopped and poked her head back into the room. "Excuse me?"

The woman—small, blonde—looked up at her and gestured to the doorway Alyssa had been headed down. "That's where the back door is, but there's a guard there. Gwenna has him posted there for applicants who are trying to get out." She arched an eyebrow. "I take it you *are* an applicant?" She gave Manhattan the once-over, as if she didn't understand his involvement, and Alyssa moved to stand in front of him, a protective gesture she didn't understand any more than anything else that had happened today.

Manhattan slipped his arm around Alyssa's waist and pressed a discreet kiss to the nape of her neck. She ignored it to the best of her ability and tried to focus on the woman in front of her. "Yes, I am, and I need to find a way out of here."

"Well, the back door is blocked." She glanced up at them for all of two seconds before she went back to her frantic stitching.

Alyssa frowned. "But how does he know who we are?"

The woman looked up at her and gave her an expression like she thought Alyssa was supremely idiotic. "Because you all look like freaking deer in headlights, that's why. He's not stupid."

Alyssa watched her remove stitch after stitch for a few seconds before she said, "What are you doing?"

The woman glanced up at her again like she couldn't understand what Alyssa was still doing there. "What are *you* doing? Get on with your own task, and leave me be."

Alyssa snorted. "Right, except I don't even know what my task is!" She waited a few breaths, and when the woman didn't respond, Alyssa asked, "Who are you?"

The woman huffed. "I'm Anna Knave. I'm Gwenna's assistant. One of them anyway." She bent back over her work.

"Why have I never seen you before?" Alyssa asked.

"Because I don't work at the magazine. I work here." When the silence came, Anna looked up again. "This is Gwenna's club. She owns it."

Alyssa shook her head in confusion. "This is *Gwenna's* club?"

"Yeah," Anna stated, "and you are beyond stupid if you didn't know that. Good luck on that job interview of yours."

Alyssa ignored the snark and picked up the end of the garment Anna was freaking out over. "Seriously, what are you doing?" she prodded.

Anna scowled and snatched the gown back from Alyssa. "There is going to be a big fashion show here tomorrow, and Gwenna's designs got messed up. The roses on these gowns were supposed to be red, but the seamstress thought they looked better white and took creative license. The *seamstress!*" She hissed the words like they were acid. "If Gwenna knew, she would have a heart attack. These are *her* designs! And they look like a bunch of wedding dresses! If I don't get them fixed, she will cut my head off."

Alyssa arched an eyebrow. "Well, that's a tad dramatic, wouldn't you say?"

Anna huffed. "She will decapitate me career-wise. I will

never work in fashion again. If I value my career, I will have all of these white roses replaced with red ones by tomorrow."

Alyssa glanced down at the pile of gowns on the counter next to Anna. "How many are there?"

"Three. Now, leave me alone! Find your way out of here. I have enough problems."

Alyssa looked over her shoulder at Manhattan, who just shrugged. She sighed and turned to Anna again. "So, do you care if we look around and rummage through some crap?"

"Do what you want!" Her voice bordered on hysteria.

Alyssa made a face at the woman behind her back, prompting a chuckle from Manhattan. Alyssa rolled her eyes and poked around, looking for—she had no idea what. She was out of great ideas, not that she really had many to begin with. Half of the reason she had even managed to make it through today was because of Manhattan.

"Hey, check this out," Manhattan's voice came suddenly.

She glanced over to see him holding up a half-see-thru unitard with bright pink sequins and feathers in strategically placed locations.

"Is it me?"

Alyssa laughed.

"Those are the costumes for the Birds of Paradise show that is supposed to take place in a couple of hours," Anna Knave spoke up suddenly. "The dancers will be coming back here in about thirty minutes to get ready, so you should probably put that back."

"This is supposed to be a bird?" Manhattan queried, inspecting the costume closer.

"It's a flamingo. There is a headpiece and a piece that goes across the shoulders and arms that look like wings also."

"A flamingo," Alyssa muttered. "How Vegas."

Manhattan held it out to her. "It would probably look better on you, love. I don't think my man parts would look particularly pleasing in this."

Alyssa snorted out a laugh. "Put that thing away and help me figure out how—" She blinked at the costume again as an idea took form. "Well, I certainly wouldn't look like a deer in headlights, would I?" She snatched the costume from Manhattan and started to tug her dress over her head.

"Um...as eager as I am to continue watching this display,

my dear, what are you doing?" Manhattan asked.

Alyssa flung her dress to the ground and turned to face him in only her black lace panties with her arm covering her breasts. "I'm getting the heck out of here," she stated.

His eyes drifted over her body. A hungry fire came to life in his gaze and he licked his lips as if he wanted to taste every inch of her skin. Her face flamed. "Dude, be a gentleman and turn around," she snapped.

He gave a playful pout, but obliged.

"Are you seriously *stealing* Gwenna's costume?" Anna shrieked.

"I'm not stealing it; I'm borrowing it for a few minutes. I'll give it back as soon as this stupidity is over. Go on with your own task, and leave me be." She fired a pointed scowl at her.

Anna glowered and then went back to unstitching.

Alyssa yanked the skintight unitard up her legs and shimmied her way into it, feeling like a stuffed sausage the entire time. She kept her panties on, even though they could be seen through the thing. She didn't know where the owner of this costume's hoo-ha had been. Gross. "Manhattan, find me the wings and headpiece," she demanded.

"Should I dress up as well?" he asked.

Alyssa frowned as he handed her the other pieces of the costume. "Why? You're not an applicant. Besides, you already look like you're wearing a costume." She stuffed her hair up underneath the rather large and flouncy headpiece full of bright pink feathers, and secured it with some bobby pins she nabbed from one of the makeup counters. When she was reasonably satisfied it wasn't going to fall off of her melon, she pulled her arms through the sheer sleeves of the wing shrug and flapped them until the pink, feathery fringe lay the way it was supposed to.

"You really do not have the body type for that costume," Anna grumbled under her breath, but loud enough for Alyssa to hear.

"You think?" Alyssa spat, whirling to face her. "Maybe because I'm not a dancer, don't starve myself, and actually have hips?" She was practically screaming at the irritating woman.

"Your body is perfect, love," Manhattan murmured against her ear.

She rolled her eyes. "You're biased."

"Maybe..." He took her by the shoulders and slowly turned her to face him. "But that doesn't make it any less true."

His words warmed her heart, and she smiled at him. She was no size two by any means, but she didn't have a muffin top or a jelly roll, she could still wear a bikini with confidence, and Anna Knave could go suck a lemon. Maybe she already had given her disposition.

"Okay, I'm over this. Let's get out of here."

Manhattan nodded decisively, and Alyssa pivoted on her heel and headed toward the back door. She didn't hesitate, just shoved it open with gusto, and the guard glanced up at her with a perplexed look on his face.

"Look, I need a smoke," Alyssa rambled off. "That cool with you, dude?"

The guard looked even more confused. "Do what you want," he said. "I'm not here for you."

Alyssa flounced past him, dragging Manhattan along behind her. She was about to breathe a sigh of relief when she rounded a corner, headed down an alley, and was met with a beaming silver reflection of teeth that made her scream. She stumbled back into Manhattan, who caught her.

"Whoa, calm down," a voice behind the teeth said.

Alyssa blinked rapidly and righted herself. "Sorry," she said before she could figure out what she was looking at.

The woman's dark face came into view, her silver teeth preceding it.

Alyssa stared for a moment, then gathered herself. "Sorry," she said again. "I just...your...grill startled me."

The young, black woman shot her a bemused expression. "Said the woman dressed like a giant bird."

Alyssa chuckled then straightened. "Point taken."

The woman put her hand on her hip. "Look, you wanna buy some weed or don't ya?"

Alyssa frowned. "Um...no. No, not tonight... Is that seriously how you ask? And why are you hiding out in a shady alley? Who's going to come through here?" She had no idea why she was engaging this woman. She should just get a move on and leave her alone. This was how people got mugged and knifed.

The woman rolled her eyes and her shoulders slumped.

She huffed out a sigh and held her arms out in a helpless gesture. "Man, I don't know what I'm doin'! This ain't even a real
grill." She tapped on her teeth. "It's gum wrappers. I only put
it on to try and look more like a big, bad drug dealer."

"Generally stoners don't gravitate toward gangstas,"
Manhattan stated, and Alyssa stifled a giggle at how out of
place he sounded saying those terms with his accent.

The woman looked defeated and she shook her head,
sending a pair of gold cat earrings jangling around her neck.
Alyssa arched an eyebrow. "The cat earrings aren't necessarily all that intimidating either."

"Look, I don't even wanna be here right now. You think I
wanna be out sellin' street drugs? I have a baby girl at home.
What kind of an example am I bein' to her? But we hafta eat.
I got laid off from my job, and unemployment hasn't come
through yet. I can't find any work. Got evicted from our
apartment, so I'm livin' with my cousin. He's the one who
sells this crap." She took out a bag of weed from her jacket
pocket and flung it down on the ground. "He told me I could
do it to get some extra cash."

"Isn't weed, like, the cheapest drug to buy? How much
money can you actually make in one night?"

"Maybe enough to get some McD's or somethin'. Food is
food, and my baby girl needs to eat. My cousin is all but useless. Just stoned all the time and eatin' Cracker Jacks."

Alyssa looked the woman over, taking in her strange yet
somehow trendy getup of black skinny jeans, Aztec print
tank in colors of black, orange, turquoise, and beige, and
gold pointed-toe shoes. Her hair was pulled up into a top-
knot, and an orange fabric headband added another pop of
color. Over her shirt was a leather jacket. "I like your outfit,"
she remarked. "No offense, but you look much too trendy
and put together to be hanging out in an alley selling reefer."

The woman beamed all of a sudden and held her arms
out. "You like it? Thank you. I made most of it myself. Not
the jeans or shoes...well, not the jacket either, but everything
else. Even the earrings."

"You made it?" Alyssa repeated. "That's wonderful work!"

"It's what I want to do, start my own clothing and jewelry
line one day."

Something clicked together inside of Alyssa's head and

her eyes widened. "Wait a second, so you can sew then?"

The woman raised an eyebrow. "Obviously," she said with a little bit of sass.

Alyssa reached out and grabbed her wrist. "Come with me." She started to tug her along behind her as she headed back toward the rear entrance of the club.

"Wait, what? Where are we goin'?" the woman protested.

"Somewhere you can make a lot more money in one night than peddling marijuana." She gave a short wave to the guard, who barely acknowledged her, and the three of them tromped back into the dressing room. A few dancers had arrived, and gave her strange looks when they spotted her in one of their costumes. Alyssa ignored them and dragged the woman over to where Anna Knave was still pulling stitches in a spastic manner. "Anna," she almost shouted.

Anna started and looked up at Alyssa. She screwed up her face. "What are you still doing here?" Her voice was so shrill it was painful.

"Look, there is no way you are going to get all of those dresses done by tomorrow. You know it, and so do I." Anna's face paled. Alyssa tugged the other woman forward. "This is..." She turned to her. "What is your name?"

The woman put her hand on her hip and gave Alyssa a look like she feared for her sanity. "Cherishe," she stated.

"This is Cherishe. She can sew. She is going to help you."

Anna looked like someone had slapped her right before she gave Alyssa a look similar to Cherishe's. "I do not have the means to hire an assistant! Besides, Gwenna would—"

"What Gwenna doesn't know won't kill her. She already doesn't know about your little dress debacle, so what does it matter? Besides, you're not hiring her. I am." She turned to Cherishe. "How much would you hope to make tonight selling...what you were selling?" She stole a sidelong glance at Anna.

"If it was a good night, maybe a hundred bucks?"

Alyssa opened her clutch and pulled out her wallet. She didn't have a ton of money, but she had enough.

Crazy that just yesterday she had been yelling at Tucker that they had no money to eat on, yet she knew she had more than enough to do this. *This* woman needed food. Alyssa didn't...hadn't for years now. She'd just used it as an excuse to justify turning her back on her dreams and wanting more things that she thought would make her feel more important.

She pulled out several bills and shoved them into Cherishe's hand. "Here's five hundred dollars. That should get you a helluva lot of McD's, huh?"

Cherishe blinked at the money like it had descended from heaven.

"This woman here is Anna. She needs help unstitching a googob of white roses and replacing them with red ones by tomorrow morning. Can you do that?"

Cherishe nodded blankly. "Y-Yeah, sure." Sense seemed to return to her and she looked up at Alyssa. "Thank you. Oh my goodness, thank you so much."

"Don't worry about it. Anna, I'm sure you could use the help, yeah?" Her tone had more than its share of bite to it. "Unless you want your head cut off."

Anna blanched again then dragged a chair over. "Pull up a seat, Cherishe. We have a lot of work to do."

Alyssa gave a curt nod, then headed back toward the door.

"That was very noble and selfless of you, love," Manhattan said softly as she shoved her way back out.

She shrugged and strode past the guard, who didn't even glance at her this time. "Just because I gave up on my dreams doesn't mean she has to give up on hers. If she does a good job, I'm sure Anna might have a few connections she can hook her up with. Regardless of how snippy she was, I have a feeling most of it was stress-induced. I wouldn't want to be on the other end of Gwenna's executioner's axe, that's for sure."

He stopped her with a soft touch on her elbow, and turned her to face him. "Yes, but the woman I met this morning probably wouldn't have given Cherishe the time of day."

Alyssa looked down, feeling ashamed and full of sorrow over so many things. "Yeah, well, like you quoted earlier, I've changed a few times since then." His gentle smile and the way his eyes filled with tenderness almost undid her; she pivoted on her heel to escape. She'd had enough emotional moments in one day to last her a lifetime. She didn't want to succumb to another one.

They exited the alley they had found Cherishe in and came out on the street where the main entrance to the club was. She walked over to the bouncer, line jumping once again, and he looked up and took a drag off of another cigar. "Who—"

"Who am I. Right. We've been through this. Look, I don't want in the club. I just spent way too much freaking time trying to get out. I just want to talk to the blond kid in there, the one who looks lost. He's Gwenna Vartz's employee or intern or something. Can you get him?"

The bouncer leered at her for a moment, then looked through the door into the club, whistled at the giant guard inside, and several seconds later, the kid emerged.

He glanced at Alyssa and raised an eyebrow. "Creative."

"Right, so I made it out of there. Wanna give me my next clue so I can keep up with this insanity?"

He shrugged. "There is no next clue."

She frowned. "Excuse me?"

"This was the last task. You're done. Now you need to see Gwenna for your evaluation. She's waiting for the applicants in the chairman suite back at the Bellagio. Congratulations. Also, could you please return the costume to the dressing room before you proceed? I will alert the guard at the back door that he is to let you through."

Alyssa stared at him for the longest time, hardly able to comprehend the fact that she was actually finished. She staggered out of the line and back to the sidewalk, then slowly turned to face Manhattan. "I did it," she breathed, more to herself than to him. "Manhattan, I did it." She looked up at him and grinned. She had actually seen something through to the end, despite the setbacks and the irritation.

He smiled at her, but it seemed a little forced. "Congratulations, love. I guess you know how to fight for something after all."

She flung her arms around his neck and held on, closing her eyes as he held her. She awarded herself a moment to bury her face against the side of his neck. He smelled amazing, like freedom and life. "Oh...thank you," she murmured. "I never could have done this without you."

"I have the distinct feeling that you can do anything you want if you put your mind...and heart to it."

She pulled away, looked up into his face—which she had come to cherish over the past however many hours—then pressed a chaste kiss to his lips. She chose to ignore the way his fingers clutched the fabric of her costume, like he never wanted to let her go again. If she thought too much on it— the same way if she thought too much on *any* of this—she had a feeling she would break down and never recover.

He still had his eyes closed when she pulled away, and the sadness in his face was palpable for all of three heart-beats. Then, he drew in his breath, stood tall, and smiled at her in the way she was used to. "Well then, love. What next?"

"Well, first I need to remove this ridiculous thing from my person." She flapped her "wings" for effect, which made him laugh. She grinned, loving the sound of his joy. "Then...I go face the big boss lady."

Chapter Ten

Across the street of the Bellagio, Alyssa stopped to stare up at the majestic casino. It was close to midnight, and party-goers were still walking—and staggering—down the street, fully caught up in their Las Vegas debauchery. It had been a day and then some, a day unlike any other days. She was beyond tired; she had been running since she got up; she had passed out and had a very real and sorrowful flashback; she had plummeted to her death and thought little of it; she had come to a hundred realizations in the smallest span of time.

And she had met a man who had made her feel alive again for the first time in much too long.

She took a deep breath and exhaled slowly, then she turned to Manhattan, whose fingers were entwined with hers. He was looking up at the casino and she studied his profile. Such a bizarre man, so whimsical and theatrical, yet so steadfast and collected. Such an adventure and a paradox. So beautiful, inside and out. She caressed the back of his hand with her thumb while she smiled at him. "Well," she said. "Ready to go?" She started forward, but was stalled by his hand pulling taut. She frowned and faced him.

He gave her a regretful look. "I'm sorry, love," he murmured. "But here is where we must part ways, I'm afraid."

She stared at him, not comprehending what he was saying to her. "What?" She shook her head. "But why?"

He glanced back up at the Bellagio and sighed. "I can't go in there. Not where you want me to go."

"Why not?"

He met her eyes and shoved his free hand into his pocket. "Let's just say, Gwenna and I...are not on the best of terms."

She felt like someone had slapped her. "Wait... You...you *know* Gwenna?"

"Well, I wouldn't say *know* exactly. Let's just say...we both wanted the same thing at one point."

Alyssa shook her head and advanced on him. "Why didn't you tell me?"

"Because you would have thought I was working for her, and you never would have trusted me!" He shrugged in a resigned kind of way. "Besides, what does it matter? She and I have never seen eye to eye, and I didn't think telling you was necessary."

For some reason, Alyssa wasn't angry when she otherwise would have been. Her mind whirled with a hundred questions about how he knew Gwenna, if he had sought her out on purpose, and so on. In the end, she didn't care. He had been a mystery all day. Why should now be any different?

She reached for him again, but he took a step away, even while he still kept hold of her hand. "Well, just come with me and wait outside."

He smiled sadly. "I'm afraid I can't, love. It's best if Gwenna and I do not cross paths, in any form."

Alyssa was unwilling to accept what he was telling her. He couldn't leave her. Not now. She turned her fear and sorrow into annoyance and rolled her eyes. "What is she going to do? Cut off your head?" she muttered sarcastically.

His sad smile graced his handsome face again, and he ran his thumb over the back of her hand almost reverently. "No," he murmured, then met her gaze. "She'll cut out my heart."

Alyssa just stood there, unable to find words. She didn't understand that any more than she understood any of this, but she felt his pain like it existed inside of her. What had Gwenna taken from him to break his heart so?

Her own heart twisted strangely. She finally stepped up to him and said, "But, Manhattan...I need you." Her voice broke with the emotions, the trueness of her words. He had been with her through everything, at her side—her companion, her rock, her sanity. How could she just walk away from him now?

He reached up and caressed the side of her face. "You don't need me, love," he breathed. "You don't need anybody. Never have." He took her face in his hands and pressed a long, lingering kiss to her forehead.

For whatever reason, it almost devastated her. There was finality in that kiss, finality she didn't want to face.

"Besides," he said as he pulled away and smoothed her hair. "If I learned anything long ago, it's this—no one can compete with Gwenna Vartz." He stepped back, gave her one more longing look, smiled, then turned and strode away.

His words resonated in her mind, echoing in an almost infuriating cacophony. She closed her eyes. "Gwenna Vartz," she whispered to herself. With his accent, it almost sounded like... "Gwenna Vartz...the—the Queen of Hearts?" She looked up, but he had already disappearing down the street. Her heart felt empty and cold.

"Who was that?"

Alyssa whirled and suddenly found herself face to face with Lindy. She stared at her for a moment, then sighed in resignation and looked over at where he had gone. "He was...the Mad Hatter," she said, her heart twinging sadly even as she smiled.

"Okay, weird," Lindy said. She sighed then looked back at Alyssa. "So, just you and me then, huh?"

"How are you behind me?"

"Oh." Lindy waved her hand airily. "I got a little mixed up with the last task. It made me late."

"What happened to Susan?"

Lindy looked surprised. "You didn't hear? She was disqualified."

Alyssa frowned. "Why?"

"She was hit by a bus."

"A bus!" Alyssa cried. "Are you serious?"

Lindy shrugged one shoulder. "She's fine, just a broken leg and arm."

"Why didn't they call off the interview?" Alyssa all but shrieked. "Give her another chance when she was well?"

Lindy gave Alyssa a look like she thought she was speaking a foreign language. "Deadlines don't wait, Alyssa," she said, wrinkling her nose slightly. "You know that."

Her words made Alyssa's blood run cold. It destroyed her to know that just this morning she would have thought the same.

"Well, good luck!" Lindy turned to face her and stuck out her hand, all smiles.

Alyssa slowly shook her hand and forced a smile, feeling anything but victorious or jubilant.

Lindy bounded away into the Bellagio, but Alyssa followed at a much slower pace. She felt heavy, burdened, and by the time she reached the chairman suite, she was all too happy to sit down on the ground in the hallway and wait for her admittance. Lindy could have first turn. She didn't care.

Alyssa pulled out her phone. Nothing. A lump of grief lodged in her throat. She'd lost Tucker, something she never would have imagined could happen. She'd taken his love and loyalty for granted. She had crapped all over it with her own selfishness. The one person who had always loved her for her, who had always been by her side, was no longer there.

Manhattan was gone. The person who had seen something worthwhile in her, who had reminded her of who she really was, what she stood for. He had boldly forced her to look at her reflection and challenge whether or not she was okay with the person looking back at her. He had opened her eyes to so many things.

Now, here she sat. All alone. She'd finished what she'd set out to do, but what did it matter if she had no one to share it with? She'd fought for the one thing that had destroyed everything she should have fought for. Her victory felt very hollow.

It seemed like an eternity before Lindy came back out of the hotel suite, and Alyssa couldn't tell if her expression was elated or dejected. She just looked...neutral.

The guard out front approached Alyssa as she was standing.

"You can go in now," he said. "Go to the conference room."

She frowned. This suite had a conference room? She swallowed any apprehension she was feeling and went inside.

Gwenna's chairman suite was lavish, extravagant, and everything that Alyssa had come to associate with Gwenna. She never settled for anything but the best. Alyssa loitered in the foyer for a while, feeling lost and confused, before she noticed movement in the corner of her eye and looked over to see Gwenna exiting from a room off to the right.

She was dressed impeccably, as always, in a tight red dress with her platinum blonde hair done up in a sophisticated yet severe chignon. She was gorgeous, the epitome of fashion, all poise and authority...everything Alyssa had wanted to be.

"Alyssa Drake," she greeted, the heels of her red stilettos clacking on the tile of the foyer. "How ecstatic I am to see that you have made it to the final stage." She offered a syrupy smile then extended her hand toward the conference room. "Please, come inside."

Alyssa followed after her, jittery yet oddly acquiescent in a way she had never been before. She didn't puff up, didn't posture in a way that would make her seem formidable. She just walked behind her, waiting for her evaluation. She didn't want to hide—had nothing *to* hide, in fact. If she wasn't good enough as she was, then forget the entire thing.

Once in the conference room, Gwenna closed the door, sat at the end of a long table, then gestured for Alyssa to sit at the other end. Typical. Ultimate intimidation. Her eyes swept over the club dress Alyssa still had on. Maybe it was entirely inappropriate for the final stage. Maybe she should have bought a different set of clothes for the evaluation, or at least put her regular ones back on.

Oh well. At least she hadn't worn the flamingo costume.

Alyssa sat, folded her hands on the table top, then faced Gwenna with no fear.

Gwenna held her gaze for a long while before she opened up a file folder and said, "My sources tell me that you have been exceptionally creative in dealing with the tasks handed to you. That is always something I like to hear."

She paused, and Alyssa sat quietly, waiting for her to continue.

"You dressed the woman...Dawn, I think her name was." She glanced down at the papers in front of her. "You dressed her differently after your initial choice. Why?"

"Because the client was unhappy, and as a representative of our readership, we need to make sure that everyone is satisfied, regardless of their background. The readers make up our business. Without their support, we have nothing."

Gwenna smirked and flipped a page. "During the last phase, you changed your dress in order to get into the club, then changed again in order to get out. Why?"

"Because I needed to become whatever would help me

accomplish my task. In the first instance, it was a VIP member of the club. In the second, it was a cast member."

"The obstacles meant nothing to you?"

"Obstacles are something to be overcome." Even as she said it, her own voice rang in her ears. For so long, she had avoided that truth, because she hadn't had the guts, the stick-to-it-iveness, the gumption. She had avoided her own obstacles because they seemed hard. Easier to bury them and pretend they didn't exist, pretend everything was always under control.

How lame was she?

When had she turned her back on everything she had stood for? On everything Tucker stood for?

On everything they had promised one another in their vows?

"I have also heard that you had a man helping you." She glanced up from her papers and narrowed her ice blue eyes at Alyssa. "There was nothing in the instructions permitting you to have help."

Alyssa held her gaze, unflinching, before she said, "There was nothing in the instructions that said I couldn't. Besides, shouldn't the position I am being offered be able to utilize a team? I know *you* do." She narrowed her eyes at Gwenna.

Gwenna sat back in her chair and regarded her thoughtfully.

"As Senior Creative Director of the magazine, I need to be able to use whatever resources are available to me."

Gwenna tapped her pen back and forth on the table top for a moment before she smirked and stood. "Yes," she drawled, while making a display of putting the file folder papers in order. "I admire your resourcefulness. However..." She closed the folder and met Alyssa's gaze with force, a penetrating icy dagger. "If you get this position, we need to get one thing clear." She put her hands on the table top, all power and composure, her eyes boring into Alyssa. "*I* am still the boss, and what *I* say, goes. You will not go off like a maverick and decide you know what's best. You will defer to me and only me." She stood tall and raised her chin in authority. "Just so we are clear, Miss Drake, you will be mine. You will be my slave. Any thought you had of a personal life will be gone. You will come when I call. When I say jump, you will pole vault. I will *not* be disappointed, or there will be consequences. If you cross me..." She drew her finger in a slow line across her throat. "I will *end* you. Do we understand each other?" She put her hands on her hips and stared Alyssa down.

Alyssa met her gaze, and for a fleeting moment, thought of Tucker, of her life, of what she had once stood for; also...what this job meant. It was the thing she had fought for, and it was the only thing she had left. A steely cold calm overcame her, and she said, "We do."

Gwenna smiled as much as she dared smile and reached her hand across the table at Alyssa. "Congratulations, Miss Drake," she purred. "Welcome aboard."

Alyssa put her hand into Gwenna's, noting the way her blood red nails scraped the inside of her wrist like talons. She smiled and nodded.

Alyssa wandered through the Bellagio in a daze until she came upon the coffee shop she had gone to earlier that day. Why did it feel like it had been a hundred years since then?

She stopped outside the entrance and looked up at the sign for a while, reliving meeting the crazy man in the hat who had changed her entire life in half a day. Warmth tickled the cold, hollow place where her heart was and she smiled. She took a deep breath, then barreled inside. She glanced around and spotted Manhattan in the far corner, drinking what looked like a cup of tea and brooding.

Her entire world exploded into light. "Manhattan!" she called.

He looked up, bewildered, then stood slowly. "Alyssa," he murmured as she crossed the room toward him.

She giggled slightly. "I thought I might find you here."

He caught her hands in his as she approached him, and his eyes traveled her face before they came to rest on her own, a question in his gaze.

She grinned. "I got the job."

She would have been a blind fool to not notice the way he retreated. He pulled his hands from hers and stepped back, keeping his gaze downcast. "Congratulations," he said softly. "It's your dream job."

She watched him for a second, then waved her hand and snorted. "Dream job, my ass. I told her to cram her job where the sun didn't shine."

For the first time all day, he looked completely shell-shocked. "You didn't?"

She giggled. "I did, kind of. Let Lindy have it. She truly loves it. I, however, do not. I never have. I'd rather have nothing and start my life over while being who I really want to be than live the rest of my life being a stranger even to myself." She chewed on her bottom lip and smiled at him. "You showed me that."

He stared at her for a long moment, long enough that she saw the play of emotions on his face go from shocked, to disbelief, to touched, to smoldering warmth. He finally stepped up to her and took her hands again. "But I thought it *was* everything you wanted," he said.

"What I really want is to not be a slave anymore. If I'm going to slave over anything..." She shrugged. "It may as well be mine...right?" The look in his eyes turned her insides to liquid. "I've spent too many years doing what I thought I should do. You helped me realize that, unless it's what *I* want, slaving over it is a futile endeavor. It's about time I stopped running from it because it's hard and confronted what I really want to do...who I really want to be. What I really want to fight for."

His smile was like the sunrise, blossoming slowly across his face and filling every part of her with golden warmth. He twined his fingers in her hair and took her face in his hands. "I am so very proud of you," he murmured.

She grinned.

He seemed to examine the texture of her hair between his fingers while his smile continued to play softly on his lips. He met her eyes and said, "There's just one more thing, love."

She frowned in question.

He pressed his lips to her forehead in another lingering kiss that turned her knees to mush, then whispered, "You're going to be late."

Chapter Eleven

"Liss...Liss... Wake up. You're going to be late."

Alyssa groaned and some of the haziness left her as Tucker's voice filled her ears.

"Come on," he called. "You have that meeting at six. You slept through your alarm."

Slowly, sense returned to Alyssa. She frowned as she recognized her surroundings—her bed, her covers, her comforter. "Mmm," she muttered, burying her face in the pillow. It was the one Tucker usually slept on, and it smelled like him. She breathed deeper. "I had the weirdest dream."

"Oh yeah?" he called from the other room.

"Mmmhmm." She sighed and burrowed deeper in her covers, unwilling to completely relinquish her subconscious adventure. "I was on the interview for the magazine job, except it was this weird scavenger hunt thing...and the Mad Hatter was there...and I think I was in Wonderland, except Wonderland was Vegas."

Tucker's rich laughter came from the bathroom. "Yeah, well, Vegas *is* Wonderland."

She smirked and nuzzled her nose into her pillow again, an odd ache in her heart. "It was...so real..." she murmured.

"Dreams always are," he answered.

With a sad sigh, Alyssa opened her eyes, and saw the austere décor of her bedroom. She made a face. Why had she decided to decorate it that way? Because it was trendy? It was so boring. Looked like someone had sucked all the beauty out of her life. She supposed someone had—her.

She sat up reluctantly, ran her hands through her disheveled hair, and reoriented herself with her life. She saw all the sketches strewn around on the bed, her empty wine glass on the nightstand. Man, she was a lightweight. Not only that, but she needed to redecorate stat. Who wanted to deal with tan, beige, and cream? Bleh...

She glanced at her alarm. The blaring invasion where she had been sucked into a tunnel. Made sense. She ran her hand over it, feeling strangely depressed and hollow at the fact that her ordeal had been nothing but a manifestation.

Well, now she knew why Tucker had never returned her texts. Guess there wasn't great signal in dreamland. She took consolation in knowing he hadn't deserted her and maybe she could still save their marriage.

She thought of Manhattan, and her heart felt heavy. A man like him should exist...for people like her. He needed to show them the truth, to show them what they were missing. He needed to make people remember what passion felt like. She put her hand to her chest and rubbed absently. She would never see him again...because he had never been real...

Tears burned her eyes.

"Hey, I have to head to the theatre in about forty minutes, so..."

Alyssa turned to look at Tucker over her shoulder, and his words dissolved. She drew in a sharp gasp and whirled around on the bed. All she could hear was the frantic thundering and tumbling of her heart as she fell back against her pillows and stared. Her hands started shaking. More tears pooled in her eyes and she labored to take a full breath.

Tucker raised an eyebrow and held his arms out to the sides. "You do remember that *Alice in Wonderland* is the play I'm performing in, right?" he asked with a slightly annoyed edge to his voice. He walked further into the room with his arms out. "I'm playing the Mad Hatter? That's probably why you had that dream. I have dress rehearsal tonight."

Alyssa wanted to scream in elation. She pulled her knees up under her on the bed as she continued to stare at him, taking all of him in. There, in all his glory, her husband stood—forest green shirt, rust-colored jeans, his eyes—one blue, one an eerie red—surrounded by bright green eye shadow on the top and bright blue underneath. The black waves of his hair peeked out from underneath a tan top hat with several playing cards stuck in the brim—one was the queen of hearts.

He snorted and put his hands on his hips. "Oh my gosh,

you did forget, didn't you? I can't even believe this."

She melted into sobs.

He blinked in confusion and his anger fizzled. "Alyssa?" Tucker rushed to her and sat next to her on the bed. "Liss, what's wrong?"

Alyssa cried ecstatic tears, and she reached up to grasp his face in her hands. "Oh my gosh, it's you." She choked on a sob and then laughed. "Of course. Of course it's you."

It made perfect sense—her draw to him, her attraction, why he felt familiar, why his kiss lit her on fire, and why it didn't feel wrong that she wanted to be with him—it had all been Tucker. He was the one who made sense of her life, the one who reminded her of who she was, the one who validated her, encouraged her, stood by her. He had always been by her side.

She laughed and cried all at the same time, nuzzling her face against his chest. She could hear the beating of his heart and she drew the sound into herself and cherished it. "Of course," she whispered. "Of course it's you." It had always been him, from day one. He'd always been in her corner—her champion, her best friend, her conscience... The fact that her subconscious had manifested him in a dream to make her get a clue wasn't all that strange. It even made sense that Manhattan hadn't looked like Tucker. She hadn't been listening to Tucker in life. Why would she have listened to him in a dream?

Manhattan had been all the elements of Tucker. He'd represented what she had been trying to ignore—her passion, her creativity, her artistry, the eccentricity she had fallen in love with all those years ago, even her lost passion for literature.

She still loved all of those things now. She'd just gotten derailed for a little while. Now, she could finally get back on track.

She pulled back and held his face in her hands, tears streaming down her cheeks. She studied every angle and plane of his handsome face, ran her hand along the rugged line of his jaw. She had never lost him. He had been beside her the entire time. "It's you," she breathed over his lips, then traced her finger along the bottom one. "Oh, Tucker." She crushed her lips to his, never wanting to feel anyone else's kiss as long as she lived. He hesitated at first in trepidation, confusion, then his arms came around her shoulders and he moaned, tightening his embrace and deepening his kiss.

Alyssa's body ignited. She allowed herself to be swept away, granting him domination as he pushed her back against the pillows and monopolized her mouth. She entwined her fingers in his hair, almost knocking his hat off, and purred her delight as he kissed her thoroughly.

She sighed against him and wrapped her arms around his neck, pulling him closer. His body felt so right against hers, so perfect. He ran one of his hands along her side; she arched into his touch. Her fingers traced his broad shoulders and chest then stopped to toy with the top button of his shirt. She fiddled with it until it came undone, then she made quick work of the rest of them, exposing his warm, smooth skin. She slipped her hand inside his open shirt and reached around to trail her fingers down his spine. He had never felt more divine to her.

He shivered a little, smiled down at her, then took her in his arms and shifted so he was sitting on the side of the bed and she was in his lap, her legs wrapped around his waist.

He kissed her languidly, like he was savoring her, and her heart filled with glorious warmth. She wanted to spend the whole evening there, kissing him, memorizing his body and everything about him all over again.

They kissed and touched for a few more moments, as if it was the first time they had ever been alone together. Finally, Tucker chuckled and retreated slightly, though his gaze remained on hers. He stared at her, searching her eyes for something. He must have found what he was looking for because he smiled softly and nuzzled his nose against hers. "As much as I enjoy this, Liss..." He smoothed her hair lovingly. "I have to get to the theatre soon."

"Can I go with you?" she blurted.

He frowned in confusion. "What?"

"I want to talk to Gerry and see if the position for set designer is still available."

His frown deepened. "But your interview—"

"I don't want it," she spat.

He blinked at her, thoroughly perplexed. She couldn't blame him.

She waved it away. "I don't want it," she stated again. "I'm not going to the stupid meeting, and screw the interview!"

Tucker regarded her for a moment, then ever so gently tucked an errant strand of hair behind her ear. "Why?" he murmured.

Alyssa looked up at him, and her heart turned over. How could she have ever disregarded him? Thrown him aside? He always had been and always would be all to her.

She took his face in her hands once more and looked deeply into his eyes. "That dream," she murmured. "It was very real. Let's just say, I was forced to look at myself in the looking glass...and I didn't like what I saw. I don't want prestige and a title, none of that. I thought I had to prove that I was worth something, but I don't need any of those...*things* I thought I did. I just need...you."

"You don't need anyone, Alyssa," he stated. "You never have."

She shook her head, remembering Manhattan saying the same thing to her. "That's not true. I need *you*, Tucker. You have always been my strength. I would be nothing without you. You're the stability in this family. Not me. It's always been you. I'm a nut-job."

He gave a small chuckle and a bit of sparkle came to life in his eyes. "Well of course you are. I wouldn't have fallen in love with you if you weren't."

While she loved Tucker's ability to find humor in most situations, she ignored it now, because what she had to say was important, and he needed to know she was serious. She tugged slightly at the hair at the nape of his neck. When he saw she wasn't smiling, he sobered and looked at her contemplatively. "Tucker, I've never known how to fight for anything. I've always just hidden, just run away. With my parents, with everything. The only thing I have ever fought for was you, and I will still fight for you. For us."

He stared into her eyes for a couple more heartbeats, then the one eye that was his natural color turned molten blue and he smiled softly at her. "Okay," he said as he pressed a kiss to her cheek. "Okay."

She choked on another sudden sob. "Tucker, I am so sorry."

"Shh," he murmured. "It's fine." He pulled back and scoot-ed her off of his lap. "Get yourself cleaned up. I have to go soon."

She nodded, and he left to go back into the living room, buttoning his shirt back up as he went. She chewed on her lip for a moment, then called out, "Tucker!"

He came running into the room in a matter of seconds. "What?" he asked in urgency.

She met his eyes and fought tears again. "I love you."

He stared at her again, like he couldn't completely com-prehend her sudden turnaround in personality, then he seemed to melt and came toward her. He tipped her chin up, leaned down, and kissed her again, slowly. "Alyssa...I love you too...so much." He explored her mouth for another few seconds before he pulled back and grinned. That grin stopped her heart. "Get ready," he whispered, and pressed an all-too-familiar kiss to her forehead. She sighed in bliss.

Alyssa headed to the bathroom, washed her face, and brushed her teeth. After that, she went into the walk-in clos-et to find something better to wear than her current yoga pants and tank top. She cringed when she looked around at all the slacks and blouses staring back at her. She was sud-denly filled with rage, and with something that resembled a growl, she started yanking all of her expensive corporate clothing down and flinging it into a pile on the floor. If she'd had a burn barrel, she would have lit it all on fire.

"Liss, what is going on in here?" she heard Tucker's voice call after a few minutes of her snarling and throwing. "It sounds like a herd of elephants..."

She faced the door just as he cautiously poked his head in. His eyebrows rose and his eyes widened in surprise. She had a Jimmy Choo shoe in her hand and she hurled it against the wall for effect.

Tucker stood there for a minute, stoically taking in the chaos she had created, then he discreetly cleared his throat and sighed dramatically. "Women," he muttered as he went over to the rack of clothing she hadn't gotten to yet. "They can never find anything to wear." He rifled through the last few articles and finally pulled out a paisley print sundress in various shades of purple, green, and brown. "I always liked this on you." He held it out to her.

Alyssa took the garment from him, and didn't even pretend not to notice the smirk he gave her as he strode back out. She glanced down at the dress and smiled to herself. She hadn't worn this or even looked at it in years. It was perfect. She pulled it on quickly and put on some light makeup. All of that and she was still done before Tucker. Actors.

While she waited for him in the hall, she noticed some pictures flung haphazardly on a decorative table that was taking up space for no reason. She really needed to redecorate. How she could even want to call herself an interior designer after looking at her bland apartment was beyond her.

She picked up the pictures and absently flipped through them. It looked like they had been taken at some kind of cast party. She didn't even remember Tucker going to a party. She had probably been at work...doing her best to be Gwenna's slave. After all, she didn't want to get her head chopped off. It made Alyssa want to laugh as she thought of how much Gwenna Vartz sounded like the Queen of Hearts. She also was beginning to think that her subconscious was more creative than she would ever be.

She stopped when her eyes fell upon a picture of a young black woman. She stared at it in disbelief. "Tuck!" she called.

He rounded the corner from the bedroom. "What?"

She pointed to the woman. "Who is this?"

"Uh...Ericka?" he answered.

She looked back at the picture and frowned. "Ericka, huh?"

"Yeah, why?" He headed back toward the bedroom.

Alyssa shook her head. "She was in my dream. Had a weird silver grill...was selling weed to make some extra cash."

Tucker's laugh echoed through the hall. "Yeah, well, that would never happen."

"Why?" Alyssa asked.

"Because she has a kid. She's super strict about that kind of thing."

Alyssa looked at the photo a little longer. "You sure she doesn't go by anything else?" she finally called. "Like...Cherishe?"

"Cherishe?" Tucker poked his head into the hallway. "No, but that would be ironic."

Alyssa frowned. "Why?"

"Because Ericka plays the Cheshire cat. Chesh-ire...Cherishe...they're the same letters."

Alyssa whirled and looked back at the picture. She stud-ied Ericka for a long time before she chalked it up to having been home at some point when Tucker was running his lines with cast members. That was not an unusual event, and she had been home for several of those meetings.

She had just sequestered herself in the bedroom and pretended not to notice.

Disgusted with herself at her blatant disregard for Tucker and his craft, Alyssa turned around and came eye to eye with the photos of them on their wedding day displayed on the wall. He looked elated, jovial, so happy it hurt.

In fact, so did she.

When had she lost sight of that?

She lowered her gaze and shook her head. No more. Tucker was the one she wanted, the one she had always wanted. She was tired of running. She was going to do what her husband always had. She was going to follow her dreams, consequences be damned. She was going to live up to her vows, not only to Tucker but to herself. She was sick of being a sell-out.

"Hey, Tuck!"

"Yeah!"

She reached up and touched the largest of their wedding photos. He had his arms around her and was smiling down at her like she was the most amazing thing he had ever seen...the way Manhattan had looked at her. "I'm going to start designing again, clothes as well as interior stuff. When I'm not working at the theatre, maybe I can see if I can ac-tually go somewhere with my ideas, do what I always want-ed. I don't want to be a journalist who is really just a glorified puppet anymore. I'm tired of having someone pull my strings."

"That sounds great, Liss," he called back. "You know I'll support anything you want to do."

She smiled. Yeah, she knew.

Alyssa headed through the living room and into the tiny

bar area they had created. It was really nothing more than a counter and a mini fridge, but at that moment, it was as good as any swanky hotel bar she had ever encountered.

She needed something to get her nerves under control, and before she had really realized it, she had pulled out all of the ingredients to make a Manhattan.

She stared at the liquor for a long while, reliving her dream and understanding just how much of Manhattan had been Tucker. Tears burned her eyes again, and she started to mix the drink. "Hey, babe?" she called. "Do you like Manhattans?"

"Of course," he called back. "They're my favorite cocktail."

She grinned and choked on a laugh, but then stopped, stunned by a sudden realization. "Tucker!" she shouted.

He came barreling into the living room moments later, looking concerned. "What is it?" he asked.

She looked up at him and let the shaker in her hand fall to the bar with a thud. "Tuck...I've never seen your costume till now."

He frowned. "O...kay..."

"No, listen!" She rounded the bar and approached him. "I've never seen your Hatter costume. If I've never seen your costume...how could I have manifested it in my dream? How could the Mad Hatter have been wearing *your* costume if I've never seen it?" Her voice took on a tiny note of hysteria.

To her surprise, Tucker remained rather still. He cleared his throat, then drew himself to his full height and fixed her with a pointed look. "Well..." He shrugged. "Maybe Wonderland is real."

She stared at him for longer than was sane. "Pardon?" she finally muttered.

"Well, I mean, maybe it's a place full of neon mushrooms and jabberwockys to a child, but maybe it's something different to an adult." His penetrating, gorgeous gaze came to rest on hers. "Maybe, it's whatever someone needs it to be when they need it. Maybe it's a place of escape...a place where one goes when they need to learn something about themselves."

Alyssa continued to stare at him, but something in his words made her heart quiver. She tried to shake off the strange feeling, sighed, and folded her arms over her chest. "Tucker, are you trying to tell me that I actually married the

Mad Hatter, and that you kidnapped me, traversed a dimension, and altered your appearance all so that you could save our marriage and basically my identity?"

Tucker glanced off to the side and scratched at the back of his neck uneasily. "Is that romantic to you?"

Alyssa considered it, then gave a half-shrug. "Yeah, actually. It kind of is."

"Then yes," he stated. "Yes, that is exactly what I did."

Alyssa burst into laughter.

"Or..."

He was suddenly pressed close to her, tilting her chin up with his finger, his body invading her space in the best way. "There is one more probable explanation...love."

His unexpected British accent rolled over her, and her body reacted with shivers and hot tingles. Her breath slammed out of her and she looked up into his eyes. She knew them...in so many ways, in ways she didn't even want to think about. Her heart hammered against her ribcage at his closeness, and at the way he grinned at her. She trembled.

"What?" she murmured breathlessly.

"Isn't it obvious?" His grin grew more devilish, more sexy, more...everything. "You're mad."

The world fell away—the real world, her dream world, everything. None of it mattered. Her smile threatened to take over her face and she pressed closer to him, enticing, provocative. Fire came to life in his blue and red gaze and she loved the message it relayed to her. That gaze of his would be her undoing, in any form, and she would happily surrender to it.

She placed her hands on his chest and looked up at him. "Well, I'll tell you a secret," she whispered, not giving one iota about what was real. She only knew that he was with her, and he was everything. "All the best people are." She let loose her best Lewis Carroll, and it had the desired effect.

His eyes sparkled with secrets and mystery, and Tucker's arms came around her—tight, confining, perfect. "Good answer, love." His lips descended onto hers, sweeping her away in his passion and his love.

She didn't care what had happened. She didn't care who he was. He could be the Mad Hatter, Jacob Marley, the Great and Powerful Oz, or a lost time lord from the land of *Dr.*

Who. All that mattered to her was that he was with her.

He was hers.

His lips were on hers and his arms were around her.

He had never given up on her, never doubted her.

He was her Tucker.

Her husband.

That was the only thing that ever would ever matter to her.

He was her Drake Manhattan.

Her home.

About the Author

Brieanna Robertson

   If someone were to ask me what I am, it could be summed up in one, simple word: Dreamer. Ever since I was a small child my imagination has run wild. I have been telling stories for as long as I can remember, creating grand worlds in my head and going on adventures that were invisible to others around me. Am I eccentric? Yes. Am I proud of that? Absolutely.

   I write about the things that inspire me, both in this world and in realms only seen with the imagination. My heroines are sassy and strong. My heroes are sometimes shy. I have an obsession with music (and musicians) and a fascination with wings. I believe true love does exist, and sometimes it is found in the strangest, most unexpected places. I also believe that family and close friends are the glue that hold people together.

Above all things, I believe in being true to yourself and seizing the day. Life is an amazing gift. Make your experience as beautiful as you possibly can.